the
white
rabbit

the white rabbit

a novel by
BRITTNEY STEWART

UNUSUAL PUBLISHING

PROLOGUE

With fists clenched, the killer waited for his chance to attack. Like any predator poised for the perfect moment, his focus was perpetual, and his heart kept a steady pace with the flapping wings of a bird flying overhead.

You belong to me – your muscles, your heart, your blood. *Blood,* he hadn't thought of that. The idea of even one speck on his freshly polished shoes was a disturbance that forced a vein to bulge from his temple, and what about his suit? He wondered briefly if blood stains could be considered a fashion statement. The man standing before him twitched nervously. The killer licked his lips in anticipation, perhaps he felt nervous too. He had gone without a kill for a very long time, and in that time his madness grew. He liked to call it madness; the most appropriate way to express the euphoria, and the immorality of his most beloved pastime.

In *the zoo*, however, this madness was accepted, and even expected in a way that pushed him to the edge. The sensation drove him to kneel toward the piece of broken glass at his feet. His prey moved then, making a run for the tree line, fear driving him away from the animal whose only purpose was to see blood fall from a victim.

The killer clutched the piece of glass in one hand, chasing after the prey – his body overflowing with adrenaline, his heart leaping with him as he bounded over the barbed wire fence. *Run little rabbit*, he thought as he spotted the shape of a man in the trees. Sunshine pouring through the canopy above lit his way, making the chase almost too easy. The man let out a desperate yell as his body landed on a bed of leaves. *Did the rabbit fall down the hole again?*

In an instant. the killer was on top of the man who wept into the foliage. Though his prey was no average man, it made little difference. Everyone in the zoo had murdered, but the killer had yet to meet a strong opponent.

Beneath the canopy of leaves he savored the moment, the prelude to his mastery. Like a kiss, the best part was not the act itself, but the seconds before – this was the hunger that drove him to raise the jagged piece of glass to the neck of his fellow monster.

-PART ONE-
THE WHITE RABBIT

ONE

Let me begin by saying that I never have bad dreams. In fact, some might say that I sleep more soundly than the average person, because I know who I am with complete certainty. I am also aware that in this life that trait is rare, so I hold on to it with a gentle, firm touch to keep it from running away.

My name is Lilith Kane, by the way. I am a recent high school graduate – perfectly situated on the edge of adulthood and childhood while trying to ignore the panic that accompanies independence on the horizon. To be honest, I don't worry about the future because I know there is a good chance that I will not live long enough to enjoy it, or to worry about it. If I am given the chance to live out my life, it will be in a cage where nobody can see me.

For the most part I am normal – if normalcy is something that concerns you. I do what I should, what my parents want, and what I know the world wants. I have put my education first, I have worked summers in fast food, and I have an interview for a new job today.

College acceptance letters have been flowing in, much to the delight of my parents, who praise me continuously. I am the perfect child, and the perfect example of what an *American girl* should be. If that is not enough, I am also beautiful.

I don't mean to sound vain, or over-confident, but like I mentioned before, I know who I am. My skin is fair and smooth, I'm thin in the dainty, graceful, ballerina sort of way. My eyes are rich and green, and my hair flows in long silky waves of copper and brown. Like my mother, I've learned to use my smile to get my way, and like my father I always get what I want.

As an only child in a financially comfortable home, I am accustomed to getting the best, but that does not mean I am spoiled or ungrateful. On more than one occasion I've been given things without asking for them, and though I love gifts, it makes me feel odd in my chest.

When I was very young my parents surprised me with a beautiful bicycle. Not for my birthday, or for Christmas, or for any reason at all apart from the fact that they loved me and wanted me to have everything. A feeling emerged from my heart and spread out in my stomach. I didn't want to be given something without asking – it was like killing a helpless animal. There was no challenge in it, and that made me angry. That is not to say I rejected my parent's gifts, I would never do that. Rejecting a gift is *extremely* tacky.

As I got older, I ran into this problem increasingly when boys tried to win my heart. For a long time I kept boxes of the gifts I had received from male – and sometimes female classmates.

One night, I took them to the river and sunk them all in a bag filled with rocks. I thought I would feel bad letting them go – the dozens of hand-written letters and pointless gifts. But I watched them sink to the bottom feeling nothing at all.

Sometimes emotions are dead to me, like a switch in my head has been flicked off and there is nothing inside but hollow, empty breath. However, I do not consider this a bad thing. I free my hand from the depths of my white duvet to test the air. My room is chilly. I had left the window open during the night, and the cool morning breeze is now flowing in behind the white, sheer curtains.

I prefer to have everything white – my bed, my walls, my curtains, my clothes. White is such a pristine lack of color, a blank slate, and a reminder of the serenity that comes with an emotionless life.

I wait patiently for my alarm to go off on the night stand by my bed. Every morning I wake before my alarm. It feels good to beat my phone to the punch on a daily basis.

Technology seems to be winning in all other aspects, but in this I am the champion. Then, as though thinking about it had brought it to life, my phone chimes a friendly tune. I quickly shut it off with a smile. Today will be a good day.

Two

"It is so cool having a new face around," the cheery blond named Hayley chats conversationally. I *despise* Hayley.

"Hmm," I mumble while I deposit a check for a well-dressed elderly lady at the counter. "Here you go, have a nice day," I smile, handing over the receipt.

"I mean, in complete honesty, Carlie can be a real party pooper, so it's nice to have someone like you around. I mean, you are just *so* likable," she continues, leaning against the counter.

"I don't really know Carlie."

"And you don't want to," she snickers.

"I don't really know *you* either," I add. Hayley goes quiet for a moment, obviously hurt. It seems she thinks we are already friends – a common mistake.

"So what are you doing tonight?" She changes the subject.

"Nothing."

"Oh my god! You have to come to my Halloween party!"

"Oh my god, I do!?" I feign excitement.

"Everybody I know is going to be there, even Joe. Ugh." She makes a repulsed face. "But you know I can't invite Chris without inviting Joe." Hayley sticks her tongue out dramatically. "But you will come right?"

"Of course," I say making a last-minute decision. This will give me a chance to meet new people, and I *adore* meeting new people.

"YES!" She squeals, throwing her arms in the air. "Wear a costume, and be there at 9:30, yeah?"

"Sure thing."

After work, I canter back to my car and go

home. The autumnal wind is forcing the leaves around; my car makes a satisfying crunch over them as I pass a few manicured suburban homes. I think about Hayley's high-pitched voice, and suddenly I wish that I hadn't done so well during my job interview.

At my parents' house I put together my Halloween costume for the evening. The decision is easy. The moment I was invited I knew what I would wear.

My well-worn white rabbit mask sits on my dresser, ready for me. I snatch my ballerina costume from last year out of the closet. There is a small, blackish stain on the midriff, but with the full skirt it is barely visible. *I should have had it cleaned*, I think. I choose a pair of dainty flats, and lay them next to my ensemble on the bed. The way the white mask pairs with the lavender top and pale skirt makes me smile.

In the second drawer of my dresser I remove a thin blade; the polished steel is cool in my hands. The handle is steel too, and engraved with beautiful roses. Including the elaborate handle, the blade is only 6 inches total, allowing it to fit perfectly in the strap behind my puffy ballerina skirt.

I shower quickly in the afternoon, scrubbing my hair and letting it air dry. After that, I style it in a high bun, tucking away any loose hairs. My parents – who are out for the evening – leave fifty dollars on the kitchen counter, which I promptly store in my tiny pale clutch before leaving.

I follow my GPS to Hayley's house feeling a rush of excitement, the blade pressing against my hip with every bump in the street. This is when I feel the most alive. This is when the air tastes a little sweeter.

Hayley's home is overly grand for someone so petty. The large open gate is made of solid iron, and reads *Green Estates* across the top in curvy iron letters. The circle drive is packed full of cars, and the house is blazingly lit. It could not be more obvious that the owners want the whole neighborhood to know about the party.

Parking half on the grass, I lock my car and check my reflection in the window. My makeup is perfect, natural with just a touch of mascara and glitter. My hair remains in an immaculate bun. I flash a quick smile to check my teeth, and I can't help but notice my own beauty – I admire it for a moment before leaving. As I am reaching for the doorknob, Hayley bursts through the door and takes me into her arms.

"EEEEK!" She makes a noise which undoubtedly triggers annoyance in everyone within ten feet. "You're heeeere!" My arm hair stands on end at the sound of her voice.

"I'm here!" I try to seem excited.

"My parents just opened up the wine cellar, you are just in time!" I try not to imagine what Hayley is like drunk. She grabs my arm and pulls me through the door, not bothering to close it behind us.

The house seems even larger on the inside. The ceiling soars to the heavens, and at the top, chandeliers dangle down, sparkling like stars. The main staircase is grand, its banisters engraved with roaring lions. The house has a medieval feel that I quite like, and for a moment I am envious that someone like Hayley should live here when I don't.

"Chris! This is Lilith!" Hayley shouts over the music.

"Hey there." Chris is a tall, dumb-looking college boy, with wavy blond hair, and a wide-set jaw. He is one of those overly muscular idiots that takes far too much pride in his appearance.

"Isn't her costume just the cutest?" Hayley gushes over me.

"Sooo cuuute!" Chris says mocking her. Hayley shoves against his chest laughing.

"You are such an idiot!" She smiles and kisses his cheek. "Lily, come check out the rest of the house!"

Is it the fact that she calls me Lily, the obnoxious pulling on my arm, or a combination of the two that makes me more annoyed by the minute? I angrily jerk my arm out of her grasp before we make it to the stairs.

Hayley seems not to notice, and continues on, yelling at random party-goers along the way. The stairs lead to a wide hallway, and then to a collection of doors, most of which are closed. One set of large double doors at the end of the hall stands open, beyond them I can see only darkness.

Hayley goes through the doors and a motion sensing light turns on, illuminating the area with a soft, atmospheric glow. I realize the room is a home-theater, and a big one at that. The red chairs, dark carpet, and floor to ceiling curtains make it seem mysterious, and even menacing. The room is empty, and spotless. It is obvious that the party has not made it this far yet.

"This is where we watch movies and stuff, feel free to come in here and watch something anytime."

In the dim light I notice her costume for the first time. Hayley is dressed as a fox, including the signature bushy red tail.

"Thank you, this is an incredible home," I reply.

"I know, mommy and daddy say they'll live here forever. They adore it."

"I understand why."

"Well, we should get back to the party!" Hayley decides suddenly. "I have to keep an eye on things."

"Of course," I agree. "Do you mind if I use your bathroom?"

"Sure, it's downstairs to the right of the foyer," she says hastily before darting down the stairs.

I make my way to the bathroom and step inside, closing the door and locking it behind me. Like all of the rooms in this house, the bathroom lacks no detail. Everything is spotless and high quality. Even the faucet is impressive. I take a moment to stare in the mirror above the sink, gathering my nerves. Touching the blade at my hip I sigh. *Now I just need to talk to people, to meet people.*

I wait for several minutes before emerging from the bathroom. Despite the number of college and high school students present, there seems to be more wine glasses than beer bottles, which gives the impression that Hayley's family has high standards for their underage drinking parties. I grab a glass of red wine and step into a crowd of slutty Halloween costumes. It is all very strange, the mixture of Halloween, red wine, and happy pop music. It almost feels like some kind of dream.

At last I see a group of guys talking in the corner. Three are dressed in disgusting horror costumes, while two are dressed in normal attire. I hold back at first, perching myself on the edge of a table, I try to look extra bored. I sip my wine and glance around the room. Within seconds one of the normally-dressed guys is headed my way.

"Hey, I'm Chad." He reaches out a hand for me and I take it.

We shake hands briefly as I take in his appearance. He is taller than me, but not overly tall, with dark hair and even darker eyes. His plain green hoodie is zipped halfway up, revealing a superman shirt beneath. A pair of rectangular glasses sit on his nose.

"Lilith," I reply. "Superman?"

"Maybe." He smiles. "Cute ears."

I take off my mask, touching the ears with my fingers. "Thank you, I made this myself."

His expression changes when he sees my face, it is the look I get all too often around men.

"Wow, really? The details are amazing. You could be an artist." He smiles, moving an inch or two closer.

"You think so?" I lean in close enough to smell his Axe body wash.

"Definitely. I mean, with a face like yours, you could do anything you want."

"You are right about that. I can do all kinds of things." I grin menacingly, and he swallows. "There's a really interesting movie theater upstairs I'd like to show you, if you want," I say touching his hand softly. Chad looks at me and nods as though he cannot believe his luck.

"Well, yeah!" He blurts out, coming off a little desperate.

He follows me like a puppy to the second floor, and down the hallway to the theater room. As soon as we are inside, he pushes me against the wall and starts kissing me. I push him away, and motion to close the doors. I start running before he turns around.

"Catch the white rabbit if you can!" I chuckle, putting my mask back on and floating down the aisle.

He darts off after me, and we make several laps around the theater before I let him catch me. I push him down and straddled him, in one quick motion, I pull the blade out of its holster and thrust it into the side of his neck. He jerks and begins to scream, but I covered his mouth and wait until he looses consciousness – it only takes a few seconds. Blood spurts from the wound and onto the black carpet, I dodge the puddle, not wanting to get blood on my costume.

"You don't hunt the rabbit, the rabbit hunts yooou!" I laugh lightly, running my finger over his blood-stained lips. I hop up and run out through the back exit of the theater room.

I switch on the garden hose, washing my hands and my blade quickly in the freezing water. Then I rush back to the front of the house and make my way back to the party. Though my heart is pounding, I keep my appearance calm. This is not my first hunt, and I will not make it my last by appearing too excited or anxious.

I find my glass of wine still at the table where I had left it – pink lipstick stuck to the rim confirms that it is mine. I drain the last few ounces and head over to where Hayley stands chatting with a small group.

"Hey giiirl!" Hayley yells at my approach. It seems every word she speaks is a shout, even though the music has calmed down.

"Lilith, this is Joe, a friend of Chris's." She shoots me a meaningful look.

"Oh hello, Hayley has told me about you."

"Oh good, then you'll know how much she hates me," he says, obviously knowing the truth in the statement.

Joe is leaner than Chris, his muscles long and slender, his eyes gray-blue, and his dark hair neatly trimmed. A thick black beard frames his face, and I spot several tattoos on his neck. He does not belong with the country-club type that Hayley and her family prefer.

"I only know that you are a friend of Chris's really," I say.

"Well that I am. And you are a friend of Hayley... and, Chad?"

My heart stops when he says the name – *he must have seen me leave with him.* "Chad?" I ask.

"Yeah, I saw you chatting with him in the dining room," he says conversationally.

"Oh, is that his name? Yeah, he helped me find a towel when I spilled my drink," I say coolly.

"We were roommates last year. Interesting dude, comic book nerd."

"That explains the superman costume." I laugh. Before the conversation can continue, I turn to Hayley. "Listen, I had an important call a little earlier, and I need to skip out."

"What!? No! Is everything alright?"

"Yeah, fine. I just have somewhere I need to be... Family stuff."

"I understand," Hayley says pouting. "But you have to come back sometime so we can hang out! I hardly got to see you!" She hugs me tightly.

"Sure," I say smiling. "Nice to meet you all," I speak to the rest of the group and make my way to the door.

The night air is festive and chilly. The music inside dulls as I make my way to the car. Nobody has screamed, and there is no sign of commotion inside the mansion walls.

It will be a while before they find the body, but I have no plans to stick around and wait for the cops to arrive. It was a risky kill, but one perfectly suited for Halloween night.

THREE

The phone call wakes me at 3:42am. Hayley's hysterical voice is blasting over my hello before I have time to understand what is happening.

"Someone died at my party!" She says sniffling.

"Wha-what?" My voice cracks.

"Someone found Chad in the theater room, *dead!*" She shouts. "He had been stabbed in the neck."

"My god. Do they know what happened?"

"No, there wasn't much evidence that we know of," she sniffs again. "I just can't believe this happened at my house, with my family and friends right there!"

"It's going to be OK, I'm sure the police will work it out."

"He's already dead, Lily!" She sobs. "The police and the ambulance just left. I feel so bad for his family..." she trails off in tears.

"I know, it's surreal. I was just talking to him tonight, and then he's dead," I whisper.

"I just wanted to let you know about all of this. I have to go and call everyone else."

"Alright, keep me posted," I say in a somber tone.

"I will. Thank you for being such a good friend, Lily." Hayley sniffs, and then the phone goes dead.

I never go back to sleep after that. The phone stays silent, and so do I. When the sun rises I am at the window to greet it – watching the golden and amber hues fill up the sky like a glass of juice in an empty cup. I have put myself in a very risky situation, one that is not typical. I have killed someone who has ties to a friend, and this makes things more complicated.

I thought I was sure nobody suspected me, but being seen with him at the party makes me worry that someone will mention my name to the police. I have no urge to be questioned by authorities, although I know I can fool them with my toothy grin, and shy girlish demeanor.

There is only one person who has connected me to Chad, and that person is Joe – the tattooed guy from the party. I have no way of knowing how clever he is, or what info he may have gathered from seeing me with Chad. Maybe I can find out where he lives and put him in the ground before he can speak against me. *But how guilty would that make me look?*

I decide on watching the sunrise a little longer before making any impulsive decisions about Joe's life. I have left no evidence, the murder weapon is with me, safely cleaned, and stashed away.

I had kissed him, yes, but that would prove nothing. It was a party after all, a dozen people could have kissed him. I am over-thinking the situation. Even if I *am* a suspect,

Hayley will back me up, and her family is beyond wealthy, wealthy enough to provide me with ample legal assistance.

The phone does not ring, and the day seems to go on as normal. I keep waiting for something to happen, for the cops to arrive and take me away, but they never do. *Maybe I am safe.* I hate letting that feeling fool me, but it's so nice to think that I have killed without consequence, and that maybe I can do it again, when the air is clear. I entertain the idea of killing Hayley and a rush of pleasure fills my brain.

The rest of the weekend I spend indoors, surfing the net and watching TV. It is best to stay out of everyone's immediate thoughts for the time being. I do the laundry, and talk to my parents, and go about my routine as normal.

Monday I will have to go back to work, which means I will be forced into close contact with Hayley, but I am not worried about her in the slightest – unless worried about succumbing to the overwhelming urge to kill her counts.

And so when Monday does arrive, I play it cool and try to ignore her when she begins sobbing on and off about Chad's tragic young death.

"He was only 22 years-old! Imagine what his family must feel like, losing someone who had so much life left to live!"

"Hmm," I mumble shaking my head. "Terrible thing." I roll my eyes when my back is to her.

"I told Chris to stop by at lunch and pick me up. I really need him to be there for me at times like these." She blows her nose. "But he insists on bringing Joe with him. He knows I don't like Joe! I can't believe he treats me this way..." I zone out at the mention of Joe.

Suddenly, I am consumed with plans of avoiding him. Joe is the one person who seemed interested in my interactions with Chad before his death. If I need to stay out of anyone's mind, it is his. Something about the way he questioned me at the party makes me afraid of him, and that feeling enrages me.

Fear of anyone, or anything, is a feeling I constantly try to overcome. Those brief moments of emotionless bliss come rarely, but they have taught me that fear brings nothing but more fear.

"Carlie, is it okay if I take off lunch five minutes early!?" I shout into the back office. "I have an appointment, but I shouldn't be too late back."

"Sure, we are pretty slow today anyway," Carlie says emerging from the room, her chubby arms full of papers.

"Thank you," I say quickly, and then turn off my computer.

"Aw, I was hoping you'd go out to lunch with us. I wanted to talk about what happened," Hayley whines.

"Sorry, later I guess." I refrain from smiling until I am outside.

Halfway to my car, someone calls me name. I cringe and turn to see Chris and Joe walking toward the entrance. I wave quickly and hurry to my car before they can stop me.

I spend the next hour worrying about whether or not they will be there when I get back. I even contemplate taking a sick day just to avoid them. With all of Hayley's droning on about Chad's death, the idea is even more tempting.

However, I know this will make me look more suspicious, so I make it back to work and through the rest of the day without incident. It is not until I am safely in bed that I relax for the first time all day. I lie there fully clothed, praying for *the feeling* to return – searching for the switch to flip that will give me peace.

I don't feel bad for killing Chad, that was the part I enjoyed the most – and I enjoyed it without remorse. But, I do feel the anxiety, that rush of potentially getting caught. this is a new sensation for me, since my past kills had been much more secretive.

My first time, I had been paranoid that someone would find out. Once I realized that nobody suspected me, everything became simple. But now the stakes are higher, people at the party had seen me. Of course, they didn't see me *kill* Chad, but they saw me with him. Somewhere in the sea of worry, I fall asleep and dream of islands and blue skies. *I never have bad dreams.*

When I wake, I check my phone to see if I have beaten the alarm. I have, but there is something else there. A text message from a blocked number pops up on the screen.

```
I know.
All about.
What you are.
Ms. Rabbit.
```

My heart stops. Questions flood my mind. *Who? How? What?* I consider replying, but think better of it. Someone knows who I am, and what I have done. *But they would have no proof!* I left nothing behind to tie me to any of the deaths. I am perfectly safe as long as I keep up appearances, and play the game well.

I stare at the phone for several minutes, my mind immediately turning to Joe and his suspicious questions about me and Chad. He had only *mentioned* seeing me with Chad, and that could have been completely harmless.

I was spending my time worrying about one potential problem, when the real threat could be elsewhere. I ponder this for a few more minutes, and then promptly delete the text message. It will do no good for anyone to see that on my phone.

If the cops question me, and look at my records, I will simply say that I thought it was a wrong number, and deleted it.

I go to the drawer and take out my blade; it will need a better hiding spot. I take the holster and fastened it to my leg, pulling my jeans up over top of it. I need to act fast, staying ahead of the enemy is my best weapon against them.

I take my bag and head out the door. I decide on a car ride to the park down town, far enough from my house to make a good disposal spot, and close enough to touristy shopping areas that if I *did* run into someone, I could use shopping as my excuse for being there.

By this time the sun is well past the horizon, and people flood downtown for work and pleasure. I make my way through the park, to a bridge over the river. This is the same location where I had dumped those love letters and gifts from so long ago.

I quickly detach the blade when I know nobody is looking and drop it in the water. The splash is silent from my standpoint, so high above with the wind blowing in my ears. I feel sad when the blade disappears, the peace I had felt destroying the letters is absent. I cannot grasp the peace no matter how hard I try. *What if they find it? Did I remove the blood properly? What if I did something wrong?* I am not ready for life in prison, or death, even though I know they are both inevitable.

Sometimes I allow myself to think it is possible *not* to get caught, but in the end I know the odds are against me. Accepting this reality is something that sets me apart from others.

I know myself – I know what the risks are, and I am prepared to accept the consequences when those risks lead to my discovery. But it is so hard to face reality when you are young, and there is so much life at risk.

The following day, I return to work but say little to Hayley. I want to keep as much distance between us as I can, though I doubt she has anything to do with the mysterious text message.

Joe is still at the top of my suspect list, but really he is the only one on my list. That night, I spend an hour on the computer trying to find out more information about Joe. He graduated from my high school, went to college for two years and then quit. His last name is Beringer, and he lives in the area.

There is no criminal record, or anything else of concern about him online. He just seems like a normal guy, no reason to suspect he should have an above average ability to notice my crimes.

I glance at my phone, wishing it would do something. I want something, anything, to happen. Sitting in the middle ground, waiting and worrying is too much for me.

And then suddenly, the screen lights up and the phone buzzes twice – the way it does when I get a text message. My heart skips again, for a moment I feel I have magical powers. I hesitate at first, but eventually I walk over to the bed and pick up my phone.

Slowly, I open the text message and let out a sigh when I read who it is from. Hayley is asking if I want to hang out with her tonight. The disappointment and relief is palpable. For an unknown reason I feel like spending time with Hayley isn't such a bad idea. Perhaps I am lonely, or desire a distraction from my worries, but nevertheless, I reply with a quick :

"Sure, when?"

I need to at least pretend like a normal person, living a normal life. Spending time with friends is a part of that. I feel strange going back to her mansion after what I did there; it seems too risky for comfort. Instead, I suggest that we meet at a restaurant and get something to eat.

"Hey!" Hayley waves me down at a small booth inside the shabby Italian restaurant she chose.

"Hello," I say sitting down and taking off my coat.

"This is so fun! We never get to hang out after work!" She has a huge smile on her face. I almost pity her.

"I know, life is just so busy."

"It *so* is. I've been trying to keep up the house now that Chris moved in, and it has been a disaster! It was so nice of mummy and daddy to let us live in the guest house," she sighs. "Did you know Chris wants Joe to move into the spare room? As if we need a roommate!"

"Joe?" I ask, taken aback.

"Yeah, he needs a place to stay, and since Chris is his best friend, naturally he came to us. He says he can pay rent, and just wants to stay until he finds a new place but *UGH*." Hayley makes a sour face and takes a sip of water.

"I understand. It was your place first."

"Exactly! I don't want to be the bad guy though. I'll probably let him stay if it's only for a short time." Hayley taps her fingers on the white linen table cloth, contemplating her situation.

I glance around. The restaurant is the kind of faux-fancy number that makes you want to roll your eyes until they fall out, and tumble dramatically into the stale bread basket.

"Does that mean he'll be hanging out with us more? You know, at parties and stuff?" I say, trying to sound nonchalant.

"Yes, I suppose he will," she says with another heavy sigh. "Wait, why do you care?"

"I do not. I'm simply making conversation," I say slowly, choosing my words carefully.

"*Hmmm...* sounds to me like you are interested in our little Joey..." She grins.

"Well, he is an interesting person I guess..."

"I swear Lily, he really is annoying. Once you get to know him you will be a lot less interested."

The waiter interrupts us to take our orders, and the conversation is lost. The rest of the meal is utterly boring – Hayley gabs on and on about the meaningless facets of her life that she thinks I should be informed of. What she did for lunch, how Chris ignores her when he's playing video games, what she bought at the mall on Saturday. Her simple mind is full of simple things that she wants to share, and I let her talk for the sake of appearances.

Afterwards, she insists on ice cream which I endure only for a scoop of mint chocolate chip, and then we part ways. On the way home I think about Joe, and how I might get closer to him. Pretending to be interested seems like a good idea. If he is the one sending the texts, I will find out – one way or the other. He probably doesn't know I suspect him, if he is indeed the culprit, and if he is not, I can rule him out.

I remain deep in thought the entire ride home, and right until I fall asleep. I hope that some inspiration will strike me in a dream, but when I wake the next day I remember nothing of my dreams.

For my lunch break at work, I sit behind the bank at the employee smoking table, alone, watching the birds pierce the autumn air with their sharp beaks and powerful wings. It is a cool, sunny day, no wind and perfect for a picnic. My bite of Caesar salad is interrupted by a man walking around the corner. To my surprise, it is Chris – he looks a little startled to see me, but recovers quickly.

"Hey, I thought Hayley would be back

here. I'm supposed to get her for lunch, but she isn't inside."

"She isn't? But I just saw her," I say putting down my plastic fork.

"I asked Carlie and she said she thought Hayley had gone back here with you for lunch," he says, confused.

"Huh, well like I said before, last I saw of her she was inside."

"OK," he pauses for a few minutes, his forehead wrinkling up in the middle. "If you see her, tell her I stopped by." He turns then and walks quickly around the building.

Hayley has been missing for over a week now, and nobody has the slightest idea where she is. It makes no sense that she would run away when she was happy with her life, regardless of the new roommate situation with Joe. I suspect that her disappearance, and my mysterious text message are related somehow. But why anyone would take Hayley to get to me is beyond my imagination. Perhaps it is not *totally* about me.

I take it upon myself, one shining autumn morning, to go chat with Chris and Joe about Hayley. I will make it appear as though I am a concerned friend in need of reassurance, but my reasoning is something entirely different. I want to know who sent that message, and why they have not exposed me thus far. Perhaps they don't have the evidence to go to the police, but either way I want answers.

When I knock, Chris answers the door in his underwear, looking confused.

"What's going on? Did you hear something about Hayley?" He is holding his hand up to block the rising sun streaming in from the open door.

"No, I was just shopping down the street and thought I'd stop by. See if you had heard anything."

"Come on in," he says holding the door open. "I'll be right back. Have a seat anywhere."

Chris disappears from the room for a couple of minutes, and returns dressed in blue jeans, and a light blue t-shirt. I suppose he is a conventionally good-looking guy, but his lack of any semblance of a brain makes his physical beauty much less appealing.

"I didn't mean to wake you up," I say politely.

"No, that's cool. I don't sleep much anyways." Chris plops down on the leather recliner next to the TV.

"I'm just so worried about her." I wipe my eyes, attempting to bring some tears to the surface.

"Me too. I know she wouldn't leave me here without saying somethin'," he says looking at the wall blankly. "If she was mad at me, I didn't know it."

"Do you think someone could have taken her?" I whisper in case Joe is home.

"Why would anyone take her? Everyone 'round here loves her. It's not like she has a ton of enemies or somethin'."

"Well, what other options are there? If nobody took her, and she didn't leave on her own, then what could have happened to her?"

There is a moment of silence while both of us think about it. Chris puts his face in his hands.

"It hasn't been long enough to file a missing person report. She's eighteen, she's an adult. The cops think she's a runaway."

"Well, we are just going to have to work harder to find out where she went."

I consider telling Chris about the text message, but I decide that is a bad idea.

"Is Joe here?" I ask.

"Nah, he stayed at a friend's house last night."

"We need him on board too, but we need to keep this hunting party small, or it will be too difficult to organize."

"Right, yeah," Chris agrees.

"Alright, the plan is this; we meet up tomorrow at the bank, where she was last seen. We will talk to Carlie, and move on from there."

"Sounds good to me. We'll be there."

"Be there at 9:15."

Chris nods his reply and clicks the TV on.

"I hope she's alive," he says quietly.

"Me too," I lie.

FOUR

Joe and Chris leave the house at 8:45am the next morning, and I am there waiting. The key under the mat is such a typical move, I feel like I am cheating by using it – but nevertheless, I have no time to waste on a break-in. I unlock the door and slide inside as quickly as possible, so the neighbors do not see. The house is dark in the early morning, the blinds are closed and the lights are off. It is dead silent, not a creak or pop touches the air as I make my way through the kitchen, and down the hallway toward the bedrooms.

I have never been in the guest house, so I don't know which room belongs to whom. I choose the first door on the right, using my cellphone as a flashlight in the dark. This room is messy, clothes are scattered on the floor, and dirty dishes are lined up on every surface. It reeks of old food, and sweat.

I crack open the top drawer of the dresser and skim through the contents. Inside, I find pocket knives, cables, and cigarette lighters – nothing too outstanding. The rest of the drawers are empty, hinting that the owner had not done laundry in months.

I push open the closet to find it mostly tidy, and full of women's clothes. *This must be Hayley's and Chris's room.* I run my hands over the colorful fabrics. The clothes are expensive and designer, typical of Hayley and her material personality. I leave the room just as I had found it, closing the door behind me.

The next room is the bathroom, it looks boring and average, shampoo, soap, deodorant, toilet paper – the usual stuff. The next room is on the left, another bedroom. The door is slightly ajar, sunlight just starting to peak through the blinds.

I push it open and step inside, this is Joe's room. Boxes line the wall in a neat row, he has not finished unpacking yet. This room is tidy compared to the previous rooms, it is clear that Joe cares about organization.

The bed is made, and he has already begun to decorate with art pieces on the walls. One large painting above the bed is particularly prominent; a king seated on a black horse, with enormous black wings and piercing red eyes.

The pair float above a burning city with a thousand faces painted into the smoke – faces mangled in pain and terror. Something about it mesmerizes me. The painting is framed in thin wood that has been painted black, and adorned with barbed wire. Joe seems to have very gothic taste – I am beginning to like him more already.

I crouch down and check under the bed, only a single antique typewriter sits there. I find it a bit odd, but move on quickly. *I am going to be late.*

I check the closet next. The clothes are

well-organized, but not all of the hangers are in use. At the top of the closet, there is a box. I pull it down, surprised by its weight. Inside there are several vinyl records, which appear to be quite old.

I place them back on the shelf and check the dresser, and then the night stand. Both are completely empty. Next I move to the boxes by the wall, and peer inside each one, taking my time. There are towels, blankets, clothes, aftershave, a record player, and below that, a wad of white zip ties. At first I don't think much of the zip ties, but then I spot something red on one of them.

I am not about to ruin any evidence, so I pluck some toilet paper from the bathroom and pick up the zip tie. It is cut in half, and a dark reddish-black substance is smeared in the grooves. I know at once that this substance is blood, I have seen enough of it to know for sure.

I put the zip tie back in the box, trying to remember exactly how I had found it. In the next box there are stacks of books, mostly average college text books, and novels. The more I look through his stuff, the more intrigued I become. Joe has serious secrets, and I am certain my suspicions are correct. *But why take Hayley?* Unless he is a serial killer too.

Maybe he knows what I am because I am a familiar spirit – something a little different than the average teenage girl. Whatever the reason, I want to know more about him. I feel drawn to his secrets like a demon to the night. I put the room back as I had found it, and leave the house, placing the key back under the mat. I race to the bank, already late by 15 minutes.

When I arrive, Chris and Joe are there waiting for me in the parking lot. I park in my usual spot, and hurry over to greet them.

"Good morning, boys," I say with a charming smile. "We have a lot to do – sorry about the wait."

"Get a late start?" Joe asks, his face giving away a hint of amusement.

"Well I don't just wake up looking like this," I say with a smile.

"Oh god, is this the time for jokes?" Chris

says angrily.

"Hey man, sorry. I just want to keep the mood light, these things can get heavy." Joe pats Chris on the shoulder.

"You are correct in that," I say turning toward the bank. "I need to go talk to Carlie, you guys split up and talk to the other employees."

Carlie is in her office as usual, absorbed in something on her computer. I sneak up to the door and stand there, seeing how long it takes for her to realize I'm there, but my patience runs out fast.

"Knock, knock," I say loudly.

"Ooh! Hello, Lilith. What are you doing here?"

"I work here."

"Not today, you don't."

"Oh, good point," I say sitting down gracefully in the chair opposite Carlie. "I'm really here for another reason entirely," I say getting serious.

"Oh? I hope you aren't asking for a raise already," she snorts. "I told Hayley no twice last week."

"Hayley is why I'm here, actually."

"I heard about her disappearance, but I'm certain she is just out on her own, taking a break from life. It's not uncommon in people your age to run off seeking adventure." Carlie types something into the computer.

"But see, that's the big problem. Hayley wouldn't run off like that. I know everyone says that when someone disappears, but it's true."

Carlie raises an eyebrow. "It does seem out of character."

"What did she say to you the day she disappeared? Is there anything you can remember. It doesn't have to be important."

Carlie ponders the question for a while. "Well, just the normal stuff. When lunch came around she took a bag from under the counter and said she was going out back to have lunch with you. I'm not going to lie, I found that a bit strange. She always goes out with that idiot boyfriend of hers."

"Yeah, I met Chris outside that day; he came around back asking if I'd seen her. Did she say anything else?"

"Well she did mention that Joe stopped by to give her the lunch bag she had left at home. Her boyfriend Chris was at work or something."

"Joe came by?" My heart is pounding.

"Yeah, I think so. I was only half listening to her, so I could have missed something."

"Well, thank you for the information. Myself and some of her friends are asking questions around the bank to see if anyone knows anything."

"I hope you find something," she says giving me a quick smile before returning to her work.

"I'm going to get out of here and leave you to it then. See you Thursday."

"Yep," she answers as I leave.

In the lobby, I find Chris sitting alone in one of the chairs near the door. "Did you find anything out?" I ask.

"Nah, nobody knows anything."

"Where is Joe?"

"He went outside to check the building, I told him I'd wait for you here."

"Listen, I need to tell you something, but

Joe can't hear about it, OK?" I say quietly, leaning in close to his ear as I take the seat beside him.

"Joe is my best friend, Lily," he says with serious eyes.

"My name is Lilith, *not* Lily," I correct. "And this is a matter of your girlfriend's life."

He looks at me for a second, and then leans closer. "OK, *Lilith*."

"I talked to Carlie about the day Hayley disappeared, and she mentioned seeing Joe."

"Seeing him where? Here?"

Before I can reply the door opens with a chime and Joe walks in. He looks at the two of us with suspicious eyes for a split second.

"Did you two find anything?"

"Not a thing," I say sadly. He doesn't question me, not even when Chris gives me a worried look. I wish idly that Chris was smarter, or a better liar.

"This is a waste of time, we should be talking to the police." Chris says.

"The police aren't going to do anything unless it seems like a serious disappearance. Right now, it just looks like she skipped town," says Joe.

"Skipped town and left all her clothes here? You know Hayley," I argue.

"Well, her car *is* gone. Maybe she felt like starting off new someplace. She has the money for it," Joe says.

The three of us are quiet for a moment.

"I don't care what you say, Hayley wouldn't leave me." Chris says shaking his head. "She wouldn't." He stands up then and walks out without another word.

"I believe him," I say looking Joe in the eyes. He seems amused by me for some reason.

"Well then, let's find her," he says scratching his beard.

When my eyes open the following morning, I am certain about one thing; Joe has to die. I had put the thought out of my mind before, simply because I thought it would look suspicious, but he is leaving me no other options. As I dress for the day, I ponder how I will do it. I would have to get him alone, at a time when Chris is at work and Joe is home. I know they have conflicting schedules which will make it easier to catch him on his own.

I pick up the phone and dial Joe's number. He answers after one ring. "Hello!?" He sounds panicked.

"Joe? What's wrong?"

"Help me, please..." He trails off – the phone goes dead.

"Joe!?" I shout into the phone, but my reply is met with silence. I throw the phone in my bag and run out the door.

I am beginning to think that Joe is not involved in Hayley's disappearance; maybe someone else is the culprit, and they have come back to take Joe too.

I push my little car as fast as it will go down the highway, until I make it to the mansion. It takes me several minutes down a winding dirt road to reach the secluded guest house at the north end of the property. Joe's car is in the driveway, Chris is gone. I jump out of my car, leaving the door open, and race for the doorknob. It's locked tight. I bang my fist on the dark oak and shout for Joe, but there is no response.

I move the mat and find the key I had used to get in before is missing. My eyes lock on an empty flower pot by the window, and before I can think twice I am lifting it over my head. I close my eyes and throw the flower pot at the window with all my strength.

The cement pot bursts through the window with ease, shards of glass spraying the ground. I knock out a few spare pieces of glass that stand in my way, and climb through to the living room. I stand there silent for a minute, looking for any sign of a struggle, any sign that the intruder is still here. But nothing seems disturbed – the house appears empty and peaceful.

"Joe!" I shout. No response.

I make my way through the kitchen and peak down the hall, taking each turn with caution.

"Lilith! In here!" Joe's voice erupts from somewhere in the back of the house. I sprint to his room and push the door open, ready for a fight. But there is nobody there.

"Joe?" I say.

Suddenly, there is a noise coming from

behind me, and before I can turn, strong hands wind around my throat. Instinctively I elbow the attacker in the gut. He cries out but does not release me, instead he falls forward using his body weight to force me to the ground.

Unable to move under his weight, I struggle to break even one limb free as I eye the room for anything I can use as a weapon. Then something pierces my neck sharply. *A syringe,* I think to myself with a gasp. Instantly, my eyes feel heavier, my body weaker. I try to turn my head for just a glimpse of the man behind me, but even moving my head seems impossible.

I fall fast into a dream where sunlight reflects on water, and leaves fall onto the surface, causing ripples to expand. I am expelled from reality – I am lost in my own mind.

-PART TWO-
ANGEL'S KISS

ONE

Observing my own physical features reflected back from the cool glass of the mirror, has always been my favorite part of the morning. My long, thin fingers fold the deep purple necktie with the dexterity of a professional. *And you are a professional, aren't you?* I think, grinning back at my striking reflection. My face is strong, but sleek, like those stunning faces that force people to buy foul-smelling designer cologne. Large green eyes, framed in thick black brows, often attract a compliment or two. My full lips combine with a strong jaw, causing people to stop and stare.

When my appearance has reached the level of perfection required for a day such as this, I bid myself goodbye, and flip off the bathroom light. Strolling in front of the glass wall that opens the living area to the pine trees outside, I notice a deer flicking its ears as it grazes – I ignore it.

"Lights on," I command as I reach the kitchen.

Soft, natural light, erupts from hidden locations behind the counter tops. I survey the cool stainless steel appliances, and sterile matching counter tops. *Perfection*, I think, pleased with my own handiwork. I stand in the middle of the kitchen for several minutes. Most men would be drinking coffee, reading a newspaper, perhaps. *Ridiculous*. I Inhale the clean smell of bleach.

My wrist watch beeps twice, politely alerting me that it is time for the day to begin. I raise the sleeve of my Armani suit and gaze at the digital time – *8:31am. Not again.*

Jerking free the leather strap, I toss the watch into the sink with a clanking noise. I am going to be late again, but the thought of leaving this mess gives me a chill that trails down my spine.

I twist the blue cap from the bleach bottle, and douse the watch thoroughly. I let it soak for a minute, and then drop it into the empty, stainless steel trash bin. This is the third watch of the month to meet its end. One minute slow is *not* perfection.

Two

The long gray hallway has a peculiar scent –
like rotten garbage masked by a spiced holiday
candle. I tap my shiny shoe against the
tasteless indoor/outdoor carpet while I wait.

"Mr. Eaton?" A short, thin woman
approaches meekly. I stand immediately and
walk to the room opposite the secretary's desk.
She flushes as I pass, but I ignore her.

The room is large, and filled with highly-
polished wood furniture. The man sitting at
the desk stands when I approach and shuffles
around the desk to greet me.

"I'm Royal O'Conner, pleased to meet you," the man introduces himself with a quick handshake.

"August Eaton," I say, returning the handshake and smiling my perfectly designed smile.

There are many things in life that I have mastered, but two talents have risen above the rest. Charming the pants off any living human being is the first. Second – I know how to *kill*.

"Please, sit down Mr. Eaton," Royal says in a manner exuding politeness. *What a chump.*

"Stunning office Royal," I smile at the nearest piece of mahogany, "does your wife give you pointers?" He flinches at the mention of his wife. *Ah, domestic issues.*

Royal chuckles, trying to cover up the crack in his shell. "Well you know women, always keen to share an opinion."

"Of course."

"I couldn't keep her out of here, she had to have her way with it." He is nervous – a curious personality trait for someone who spends his time in the presence of celebrities and millionaires. I notice that he moves then, to touch his bare ring finger. *Why would he lie about his marriage?*

"Moving forward with this meeting, I've brought the script you asked to see. *Revised.*" I pluck the script from my leather bag, and place it on the desk. "It's going to blow their minds."

Royal hesitates at first, and then pulls the script toward him.

"So glad you took the time to come in and discuss this." He flips through the pages slowly, though he appears to read nothing of the words written on them.

"If you have any specific requests, don't hesitate to call. I'll be more than glad to make small changes to accommodate the actors. However, any length added to the script will increase my fee."

"Of course, of course," Royal murmurs, still flipping the pages. "Well then, fifteen thousand in advance, the rest upon completion of the film?"

"Sounds like perfection," I say grinning.

"Good. Listen, Mr. Eaton, there is a party

tonight, strictly for those involved in the film. What do you think about stopping by?"

When opportunity knocks. I pause in short, giving Royal the chance to think I am unattainable. "I would be glad to, sir."

"Great!" Royal is nervous again. "It will be in the Lobby, eight o'clock."

For the rest of the meeting we run through the paperwork, and I sign the agreement. When it is time to leave Royal seems to relax. *He is definitely intimidated by me*, I think as I drive across the curvy roads of the city. *Understandable.*

When I arrive home, I immediately go to the closet. This is a big night, not only am I obliged to charm my bosses, but tonight I am *hunting.* Most people do not understand the true art of the hunt, but I am proud of my rare abilities. I run my fingers along the silk vest – closing my eyes – appreciating the sensation. *The perfection.*

That night, when I am dressed in the red silk vest and black suit, I tie the skinny black necktie, and apply the finishing touches to my casually tousled hair. I carefully cover the scar just under my hairline with a piece of hair.

I should be angry about the scar, but I'm not. I become aware in this moment of reflection, just how patient and gracious I am. After all, the scar is just a casualty of art. Surely one cannot go forever without taking a bruise for their passion.

When I arrive just after eight-thirty, I am feeling refreshed, and prepared for the events that will surely take place. The air is full of promise and the sickly stench of wealth. People watch closely as I make my way into a crowd of thin, attractive women, and old business men.

"August!" A voice surges through the crowd. Royal is waving his hand, motioning for me to join him in a circle of people.

"Good to see you again, Royal." I shake his hand.

"Wonderful th-that you came!" Royal stumbles over his words, frazzled by my very presence.

"Thank you for the invitation, sir." I feel

my powers working. All eyes are on me, wondering who I am, and how I know the producer – the squat, toad-like man standing next to Royal.

Royal is just starting to introduce me to the elegant and wealthy members of the circle, when suddenly, I notice a woman. Small and thin, she is perfection in its purest form. The hunt has already begun, and I had almost missed the sounding trumpet.

"Excuse me, sir. I think I will buy that young woman a refreshment."

I give Royal no time to reply as I head for the bar where the woman sits perched like a dove on a wire. I admire her before making an approach; her delicate frame is veiled in a sheer golden dress that dips down in the back, revealing warm, olive skin. I take note of her impeccable taste, her shoes match the exact shade of gold in her dress.

I sit down beside her and watch her sip champagne. Her hands and arms are spotless, not a scar or freckle marks her complexion, and her face is much the same. Her hair is carefully braided and twirled into a bun of absolute transcendence. She turns to me finally, noticing her new admirer with amusement.

"Can I help you?" She says in a toasty, clear tone. Her voice reminds me of a summer day. *Oh this will be a challenge.*

"No, don't mind me." I grin irresistibly. Her eyes brighten. *She likes me.*

"But you are staring at me, it's unnerving," she whispers, leaning closer to my face. I examine her expression closely, her eyes are flawless as well – pure green, without a fleck of brown or blue. Her nose is perfectly symmetrical, and her lips...

"I'm trying to find a flaw in you," I whisper back. She smiles despite herself.

"That can't possibly work, can it?" She laughs musically.

"I'm sure I don't know what you mean." I keep my face a perfect mask, humorless.

"What I mean is that you expect me to fall madly in love with you, simply because you say I'm perfect. Tell me something I haven't heard before." She looks back at me with the same intensity I am giving her. *Ah, a tough one.*

I look her over again, stopping on the hand that holds her half-empty champagne glass. *She is shaking, I am affecting her.* I smile, allowing my radiant appearance to fully shine.

"You are nervous around me," I say touching her shaky hand. She seems insulted, and moves her hand away.

"I guess it does work after all," I say, rising from my seat.

She attempts to ignore me, but her body language changes. *She is upset that I'm leaving.*

"It probably doesn't mean anything to you, but it wasn't a trick. I really am looking for a flaw in you. You are perfection."

I turn then, and walk into the crowd. I don't have to look back to know that she will follow me. I have done this so many times before, it is simply part of the hunt.

In all of the years I have spent honing my skills, I have made very few mistakes. I always come back with at least one fish on the line. This night is no different. In fact, the fish need no reeling in, she is more than eager to follow me wherever I want her.

I make my way to the entry hall where the two glass doors open to a small garden. I step out into the cool night air, and wait for a moment, making sure that I do not to lose her in the crowd. When sufficient time has passed, I set off, strolling through the shadowy garden.

It is dark enough that I cannot not see if the flowers are red or purple. In the penumbra, I find a beauty far beyond the simple colors of spring. It is this quiet emptiness that I crave. In the dark, I feel a moment of peace that comes about rarely.

I am surprised to find such a moment in the middle of a hunt, but I welcome it nonetheless. I close my eyes and let the breeze brush across my face. It feels so intimate, like the night knows me more than anyone – it whispers something I cannot understand.

"Perfection isn't everything," says a voice from beside me. "There is as much beauty in imperfection, if not more." *Hypocrite,* I think without opening my eyes. How could someone so beautiful say such a thing?

A few seconds of silence later, I open my

eyes to find her sitting beside me on the iron bench. I do not recall how I came to be here, the thought of this troubles me. I face her, but her eyes are on the moon.

"Why would you say that?" I whisper.

"Because, perfection is only an *idea,* not a reality." She turns her gaze from the shining moon, to me. Her eyes look black in the darkness, I long to see her for what she is before the hunt is over.

"Let's go for a walk," I say, taking her hand. She obeys without question, a mistake too often made by unknowing victims.

We make our way down the dimly lit path, through the trees that line the garden. I hold her hand firmly. *Such lovely hands.*

"Do you believe in angels?" I whisper only to her.

She hesitates at first, confused surly by the randomness of the question.

"Yes, I think I do," she says.

"I never thought they were real, until now," I say and she blushes under the dim lamps, holding my hand tighter.

It is my job to make her feel comfortable

with me, to make her *trust* me, to adore me instantly – I am succeeding on every front.

Then, I know the time is right. I stop, forcing her to stop with me. I do not let go of her hand. She looks at me, puzzled.

"What is it?"

"I have to find out for sure," I say moving closer. She does not back away, she longs to be near me, I can feel it. Suddenly, I push her against one of the old trees, kissing her hard. She tastes like champagne and strawberries, even in this she is perfection.

At once, she pushes me away. I stagger back in shock. I have never been rejected before. I advance on her again, this time throwing her to the ground, covering her mouth with my hand. I press hard so she can't bite, and I move my face closer to hers.

"Angels don't bleed, you see, I have to make sure, I have to check." Her eyes are wide as she screams into my hand, a weak, pathetic sound. I feel a rush of adrenaline – the hunt is over, the prey has been captured.

THREE

The photograph was beginning to crinkle in the hands of the sleeping man. In the eight years since it had been taken, the picture had yellowed around the edges, but the young boy's face was as clear and beautiful as the day he died.

My name is Royal O'Conner, and that photo is of my son. I was a single father when my child was murdered by August Eaton. The devastation had been so overwhelming – to have your only real family ripped from your hands... Because of August Eaton, there is a constant ache that will live in my heart always. I wake up to the sound of a revving engine, and carefully store the old photo back inside my suit pocket. I look around for what I might have missed while I was sleeping.

It is August again, pulling away from his upscale home in a new BMW. I feel sick thinking that someone so demented should be so successful. Everything and anything he desires is his to take, including human lives. I attempt to reign in my rage as I start up the car. A bead of sweat travels down my cheek.

I always spend my mornings like this, I am an obsessed man, and well aware of the fact. You would be obsessed too, if you knew the man who killed your only child. Not only do I know him, but for years I have had no way of proving August's evil nature.

I tighten my hands on the steering wheel as I follow August into a middle-class neighborhood. *What does he want with these people?* In all of my time observing Mr. Eaton, I have never seen him associate with anyone under $200k per year.

August whips his black BMW into the

driveway of a two-story brick home. Knowing better than to park too close, I circle the block and find a spot at the end of the street, barely visible from the house.

August is surprisingly unobservant. However intelligent he may be, he is also exceedingly arrogant. This personality trait is an asset that I take advantage of whenever I can. In all of his haughtiness, August will never suspect that anyone would know what he truly is.

I watch as he casually strolls up the stone path to the house, like he owns it himself. He extracts something from his khaki pants pocket and opens the door. Before I can process my confusion, August closes the door and disappears from view.

I count the time on my car's dashboard clock. *What is he doing in that house?* Thirty-five minutes pass before August emerges again, this time he is holding a briefcase. August tosses the case into the passenger seat of his car and backs out quickly.

Back at the office I wait for news – It seems that's all I ever do on days like this, when work is slow. Though I do a lot of the investigation on my own, I am not always available to watch August. After the incident at the party, I am afraid we might lose track of him again.

I keep telling myself that August is oblivious, but I find it suspicious that at the very moment we lose track of him, somebody disappears. That party was no different – if we hadn't lost him in the garden, maybe we would know what happened to that poor girl, and maybe the cops would have enough proof to put August away for good. That is exactly where he needs to be – *monsters deserve to be caged.*

The day goes by without event, and I am starting to feel discouraged. I drag myself home after work, I couldn't bare another night of watching August lock his doors and check them twice, or another moment of staring at the blank windows, knowing *that* creature is sleeping soundly inside.

Of course, I will not let August go free, I am still as determined as ever to catch him – but I have private investigators for that. Turning on the lights, I throw my keys on the kitchen counter, and ignore the thought of food, instead going straight to the computer desk. I spend most of the night exchanging emails and texts with the PI's, even though I stayed home to take a break from the investigation. I can never *really* take a break from my mind, however, as the night goes on I know that staying home is not an option. Waiting around the house while others do my work makes me feel sick.

Before I know it, I am back in the car, and parked down the street from August Eaton's dark dwelling. It is funny, in a way, to think about how a house reflects on a personality. The dark windows, cool steel, and simple lines, perfectly illustrate the exterior of the cool criminal living inside.

I often wonder if the inside of August's home is as demented as his soul. And then, as if the simple thought was drawing him out,

August appears. I lean forward for a closer look, thinking maybe my tired eyes are fooling me.

August Eaton is there, standing outside, bathed in moonlight and completely naked. As he walks to the nearby garage, I notice patterns on his skin – dark shapes swirling into an unreadable collage.

August acts as though this behavior is completely normal, and does not spare a glance around the neighborhood. Instead, he walks straight to the garage, disappearing into the darkness. I sink down into my seat, hoping that I'm not visible from the garage. The clock on the dash reads *3:15am.*

The neighborhood is completely silent, and since most of the neighbors are retirees, this is not a surprise. What is surprising, however, is when August emerges again from the garage.

He has put on clothes, though the strange marks are still visible on his face and arms. He is carrying two black bags, one in each arm. I fumble quickly for my phone, and when I finally push the record button, August is throwing the plastic bags into the back seat of his BMW.

Before I can stop the recording, August turns to me as though he had known the whole time that someone was watching. I freeze, phone in hand, praying that the darkness conceals me.

August turns then and saunters back into the house, not looking back. The lights in the house remain off – *perhaps August has night vision,* I think, turning off my phone.

Four

The darkness is such a beautiful blanket, and how I wish I could be buried in it forever. Perhaps I could – perhaps in death I would be covered by the safety of night for all eternity, but that thought is passed away hurriedly. I thrive in this world, and the world needs me.

My unique qualities, and unconventional ways, must surely cause onlookers to understand a little more about the meaning of life. I wait in the dark with my eyes open until the sun peaks through the window, bounding off the walls, and onto my smooth, gray ceiling. I run a hand across my chest, the dried blood flaking beneath my fingers. The feeling is bewitching and free, like the empty cage left behind after a bird has been set free.

I revel in it, absorbing the feeling of empowerment. I have set the bird free, nobody should be allowed to cage perfection. And oh how beautiful she was – *so breakable.*

I roll out of bed and pick up the plastic that lines the mattress. The bathroom mirror is once again, my only friend, and I would have it no other way. I stare with quiet interest at my own reflection. The man in the mirror is shirtless, hair disheveled, and his entire body is covered in a birdcage-like drawing. The dark streaks across his chest are applied not in paint, but in blood.

It is the blood of the beautiful women, the angel. I have set her free, and certainly somewhere in heaven or hell she sings my praises. I push away thoughts of the freed angel; I should not let my mind stray from the night previous. Someone had been watching, and I recognized the car.

Since nobody has ever suspected me of my

crimes, this is a major hiccup in my zero suspicion plan. Not to mention, I had been naked, and covered in blood that particular night. How would I explain such bizarre behavior if it came down to it?

Perhaps I would say that I had been locked out of the house during a wild party – but then, my neighbors never saw people over, or heard music. I am aware of my reclusive tendencies, and I know that the neighbors notice as well. When I do bring someone home, they are never *lively* guests, if you know what I mean.

I decide to dress, and go about the day as normal, though the sinking feeling never quite leaves. *Could it be possible that someone is watching me? How would anyone have caught on to the things I have done?* I always keep careful watch, making sure nobody notices, or suspects a thing. *Could it be possible that someone has been keeping just as close of a watch on me, as I have on them?*

As crazy as the idea seems, I cannot go on enjoying my life, or my work, if I do not find the answers to these questions. Having decided to walk, I take to the streets – my newest pair of shoes shining in the sunlight. The day is as normal as any other, and I feel a twinge of annoyance at that fact.

It is a glorious tragedy that human kind could be so diverse and expanding in both knowledge and population, and yet remain so normal and plain. As I walk I watch for cars and people, things that I never bother to see unless I am going on a hunt. There is never a reason to pay attention to such insolence when it causes you no harm – *at least that's what I thought.* As if on cue, I hear the revving of an engine somewhere behind me, but I do not turn. *This is my watcher,* and I insist on staying one step ahead. So I walk on as if I have a purpose.

When I have walked long enough to find a shopping center full of overpriced boutiques, I slow the pace and look for something my style. The sign reads "*Franklin & Harvey*" in classic swirling font. *Bickham Semibold,* I think to myself with a smile. That graphic design class wasn't useless after all.

Though the door chimes politely as I enter

the shop, none of the employees greet me. In fact, the store seems quite empty. The sound of soft music plays from somewhere above, and the scent of vanilla floats past, begging me to come in and buy something – *anything.*

I peruse the neatly organized dress shirts and wait for something to happen, allowing my instincts to lead.

"Can I help you?" A women speaks from behind me, I do not flinch, or even move to look at her.

"Just looking," I reply back, and there is a moment of silence before she speaks again.

"OK, just let me know if you need anything." I can hear the disappointment in her voice, it must have been a long time since her last customer.

When I am half-way through the second song on the radio, I leave the store and walk back out onto the street.

In the reflection of the shop windows, I notice a tan Lincoln pulling to a steady stop at the curb. I am certain that this is the same car from the previous night. My insides leap with excitement. *This is going to be fun.*

I lead my prey to the exact place I want him to be. Past the boutiques, and into a near desolate parking lot. I circle around the back of the decrepit super market and wait patiently behind a pillar. The gate to the back entrance is locked, so the only way for my watcher to follow will be down the side alley. This will make for a perfect opportunity to catch my prey by surprise.

I stand unmoving next to the peeling paint of the pillar, and slowly but surely the sound of an approaching car makes itself known. It seems like several minutes pass before the car stops. I crouch and lean around the corner near the chain link fence.

Further down the alley sits the used tan Lincoln, a man is inside, too far away for me to see him clearly. I lean back and think through my options. Coming to a quick conclusion I stand, straighten my tie, and step out on the sidewalk, toward the front of the super market. I keep a causal stride, looking straight ahead, giving the impression that I know where I'm going and for what purpose.

The car revs back to life instantly as my

feet hit the sidewalk. The driver quickly pulls away. I get a good look at the license plate and smile.

FIVE

The child's eyes are focused hard on the fountain. Time passes slowly as he sits on the park bench, watching the water shoot up to meet the sky, and then as it falls back down, splatting against the damp cement. He could be no older than 8 years-old, but even in youth his perfection is unmatched.

The boy has eyes as bright blue as the sky above him – his skin pale and clear. His hair is carefully maintained for someone so young; I assume his parents have something to do with this. They are also responsible for the child's sadness. It is clear that the boy desperately wants to leap into the fountain where the other kids are splashing and playing.

Every few minutes the boy looks back at a man chatting with his companion. This is surely the boy's father – a prideful, polo-wearing soccer dad. I make a move to approach the child, but I stop myself, settling against the side of *Pizza and More,* where I am less visible to the boy's father.

A gust of wind blows through the terrace, pushing a piece of hair into the boy's eyes. He quickly swipes it back in place and holds it firmly for a few seconds before letting go. Perhaps I am wrong – maybe the child *is* responsible for maintaining this appearance, or maybe a lifetime of expectation has taken its toll.

"Parker!" The child whips around to look at his father. "Come on, time to go home."

Before his father has even finished the sentence, the boy is on his feet and running. As the wind catches him, he puts a hand on his thick brown hair to keep it in place.

I watch them disappear beyond the entrance of the terrace before making my move. Last time I had missed the opportunity, but now I am prepared. I walk behind the over-priced pizza arcade, to the motorcycle I had parked earlier in the day.

I see the two just as I round the corner. The father opens the door for the boy and waits as he climbs inside. The moment seems to drag on forever; I itch to get on with it. When we are finally on the road, I feel no better. *What if something happens before they get home? What if there is a car accident and the boy is...damaged.*

I weave in and out of rush hour traffic, keeping a safe distance from the silver sedan. Finally, they wheel into a cul-de-sac. This is a crucial moment for me – everything must stay on schedule.

First, I will park the motorcycle far from the entrance, so that nobody can see me leaving the neighborhood during the night. I will make the trek back to his house on foot with my backpack in tow.

I am careful to climb over the wall and

enter the neighborhood from behind. I give myself a bit of mental praise for being so cautious. I cannot deny the fact that my intelligence is above that of the average man, and so completing this job will be simple. I have no doubt that this time everything will go smoothly, and I will be made stronger by it.

Six

I rinse my face in the bathroom sink – my hands are still shaking when I get a glimpse of my tired eyes in the mirror. It had been so close, August had almost seen my face. I cannot let it happen again, everything I have worked for could have been lost because of one careless mistake. The bold truth is this; August Eaton is a killer, and he deserves to be caught. But how can I catch him if he is so aware of my every move? I have made a big mistake by getting too close, and getting close to someone like August means danger.

I settle into my computer chair late that night with quiet anxiety. It feels wrong to sleep after having a run-in with someone so despicable. But it is not long before I doze off at my desk again – this is something that happens frequently. My dreams are full of mixed images and memories of my long lost son. A knock on the door rouses me from my sleep.

I freeze, contemplating in my half-sleep state whether or not to open the door. *I am not expecting guests.* I lean against the door frame and wait. Two more knocks. I look through the side window and see to my horror that August Eaton is boldly knocking on my door. I panic, a thousand options flying through my head.

Should I open the door and pretend to know nothing? Should I ignore him altogether? I am struck with the realization that August is getting into my house whether I open the door or not. I run to the desk and pick up my cell phone – a battered and bruised touchscreen with a chunk missing from the glass.

Just as I turn the phone on, the door bursts open. Without even looking at the intruder, I climb the stairs toward the bedroom where I keep my gun. I refuse to look back as I reach the room, slamming the door shut behind me. I lock it instantly, and with precision; I had planned for this scenario a hundred times.

I pull the gun out of the top dresser drawer, and flick the light switch on and off three times. The doorknob rattles and then stops. I brace for an attack – for the door to fly open, and the man who killed my son to be right there in front of me; but nothing happens. The room is dead silent. Seconds later, I hear voices downstairs. The men I had hired to watch my place tonight saw the flickering light in the window. I approach the door and carefully unlock it. I step out into the hall as quietly as I can, holding my gun high.

"Sir, are you up there?!" A voice comes from below.

"Here!" I call back. There is no sign of August Eaton anywhere.

The two men meet me at the top of the stairs. I motion toward the guest bedroom on the right; checking each closet and corner along the way. The bedroom door is cracked open where it was previously closed.

I am certain that August had decided to hide when he heard my men coming into the house. Perhaps three against one are not the odds he wants. Slowly, I push open the door and look inside. The window is wide open and the room is empty. I check the closet, but there is no trace of my intruder.

"He's gone," I say, defeated.

"Sir, you shouldn't be here," one of them says.

"We have to find him."

I am filling up with rage. In this moment I am ready to kill August Eaton – ready to put a bullet in his face for the things he has done.

By breaking and entering, he has given me the perfect excuse to do so. But August has escaped me. I peer out of the open window and see the tree August used to climb down. There would be no way to catch him on foot, August is an experienced killer, and a clever one at that. He knows the area, and he knows exactly how to escape.

I slam my fists against the window frame, pain shooting up my arms. It seems like no matter how close I get, August is one step ahead of the curve. Even when I think I have the advantage, August still keeps his head above water and out of my grasp.

The sudden attack, however, makes me reconsider exactly how bold he can be. Part of me wants to remain in the house and wait to see if August will come back. But he is not an average criminal, he is smart, and I am more than aware of the fact. I have no way of knowing what he will do now.

I decide on changing tactics. At the urging of my hired guards, I call the police and report the break-in. The police assure me that the place will be watched, and that August will be caught and questioned.

Of course, I know better than to believe that. Years of research and careful planning, and there is still no link to my son's murder.

Despite every setback that should have discouraged the mission, nothing will ever keep me from my goal. I had made up my mind the moment my son was taken from me, and nothing can redirect the feral need to see August Eaton punished.

While the police watch the house, I will have to make a move on August before he gets away. There is no doubt that he will try to run, now that he knows he is being watched.

I set out for August's house feeling anxious. I am certain that August will not return home after the police have been informed of the break in, which will give me the opportunity to check the place out. The house appears empty when I arrive – just as I had suspected. There are no lights on inside, and the garage door is, unfortunately, closed.

I park down the street and walk through the cover of night, so the neighbors cannot see. I make my way to the back of the house where the gate to the wooden fence is unlocked. I look through the window at the back door, and find the laundry room empty. The pristine washer and dryer look brand new and unused.

A row of empty laundry baskets are neatly stowed against the wall nearby.

I put my jacket against one of the glass panes, and removing my gun, I thrust the hilt against the glass. It shatters, and pieces of glass fall inside. I reach through the empty frame and unlock the door – being careful not to snag my wrist on the glass fragments.

There is a silent alarm in the house – I know this from a past dig through August's garbage. If it goes on for too long, the police will arrive, but I came prepared. I promptly enter the security code as soon as the door is closed behind me. The system beeps once and then a light above the keypad turns green.

The house is dark, but I check every space where the moonlight does not touch – where the shadows reign – but there is nobody hiding. I am not surprised by this, I did, after all, suspect that August would not return home here, or to his second house for fear of being intercepted.

From what I can see of the dark rooms, the house is spotless. Everything is in its place, giving the impression that nobody lives here. I check the refrigerator out of curiosity. I cannot imagine someone living in a house so untouched.

The light from the fridge pours out onto the counter tops behind me, but I don't worry about the officers parked out front seeing it. There are exactly two cartons of orange juice, and two eggs inside, both neatly placed side by side. I half-expect to find severed heads in the freezer, but when I look, there is nothing at all.

I don't bother with the rest of the kitchen; instead, I go to the bedroom where the door is closed ominously. Before I can open the door, something catches the corner of my right eye. The bathroom door is open, and I can hear something dripping inside.

I try to stay calm, but the gun in my hand is shaking. In my imagination, I see a severed torso hanging from the ceiling, blood dripping into the bathtub. Slowly, I walk inside and flip on the light.

The bathtub is empty, and the faucet is leaking loudly onto the bottom of the tub. I laugh out loud, letting the gun rest at my side.

I cannot believe I let paranoia get the best of me.

I turn to inspect the mirror. Everything is immaculate and organized, just like the rest of the house. All of a sudden, through the mirror I see the door swing forward, and August is standing right behind me, shirtless and covered in blood, like some grotesque nightmare.

Instantly, I turn the gun to the maniac, but August is faster. He twists my arm backwards, swinging his own arm down on top of mine with incredible force. The bones snap loudly and I cry out into the dark house – the pain is filling up my brain and overflowing. I lose grip and my gun falls, hitting the tile hard. Before I can move, August has his hands around my neck, squeezing until we both fall to the floor. The pain has me momentarily blinded, and when my sight finally returns, I see August on top of me – his blood covered face splits into a huge grin. *He thinks he has won.*

The lack of air sends me into a panic. I use my good hand to reach behind my body for the pocket knife clipped to my belt. August is so consumed with the joy of strangling me that he doesn't seem to notice when I pull the knife out and push the blade free.

With all the force I have left in my oxygen-deprived, pain-ridden body, I thrust the blade into August's thigh where it sinks up to the handle.

August lets out an insane sound, like a pig at the slaughter – wild and desperate. He falls sideways away from me, wailing. I make a move for the gun on the bathroom floor.

I recover the gun, and turn to see August pulling the knife out of his thigh. He stands with the knife in his hand, ready for a fight – but he stops when he sees the gun; his manic smile fading.

"This is where it ends," I say to the animal before me. I have finally captured the beast. *This man killed my son.*

Suddenly, a sickness fills my stomach – a heart dropping despair slides down my throat. I keep the shaking gun fixed on August. *I broke into his house. I stabbed him. I have no proof to support that August is a murderer, or that he is anything but a trespasser.*

This lack of evidence prevents me from killing him. *I need proof to lock him away. If I kill him now, I am going to prison.*

"Ticktock," August says smiling through the blood on his wicked face.

I keep the gun pointed at him while I reach for the cellphone in my pocket. As my heart races, the phone rings – August makes no move to fight back.

"We have to find a way to get rid of him." Anthony, the more mild-mannered of the two men speaks over the bar music.

"I know that, but how?" I say.

"I know some people," the other man named Darryl whispers.

"It has to be something safe – nothing that can lead back to us." Anthony takes a sip from his beer as though the action is a punctuation point. He does this a lot.

"When I first started this job, I met a guy named Beringer. His whole family owns this operation that disposes of criminals like Eaton," Darryl says leaning closer to me.

"You mean he *kills* them?" I whisper the word.

"Nobody knows what they do with them, but I'm going to go out on a limb and say yes, he will die." Darryl leans back in his chair – it squeaks sadly.

"I have to know that August will get the punishment he deserves," I say.

"We don't have many other options now that you've screwed everything up, do we?" Anthony says getting irritated.

I know he is right, but I feel angry at the finger-pointing. Nothing is working out the way I want it to – the way August Eaton deserves. My options are running thin. I could kill August myself – enjoy it thoroughly, and hope I don't get caught. Or I could let Darryl's contact take him. I have no way of knowing the outcome of that option.

"We need to head back soon, so let's make a decision, eh?" Darryl urges.

"What if we go with this Beringer guy, and August ends up back on the streets? He would kill us all for this," I say seriously.

"Like I said, we don't have many options. I

say take the chance." Darryl shrugs.

I nod, though my insides churn at the thought of letting August go alive. We hurry back to my basement, where August is still unconscious from the drugs. He is tied tightly to one of the support beams, barely even breathing.

Darryl makes contact with the Beringer man, who agrees to take August out of our hands. I urge Darryl to question the man about his plans for August, but Darryl simply says that he is not to be questioned, and leaves it at that. The three of us take turns watching August during the night; administering drugs as needed to keep him sedated.

I am on edge – both relieved and unhappy. The idea that I may never know what happens to August Eaton in the end, almost makes me feel worse than knowing he is alive and living in the same city. At least then, I would be able to keep an eye on him, perhaps even see him behind bars.

But it is too late for those fantasies. The

only thing left is to accept the way life will be without my biggest obsession. Before I can work out my emotions, there is a knock on the back door that makes us all sit up. I stand quickly, and open the door.

There is a tall, bearded young man on the other side. He is not at all what I had expected the mysterious Beringer to look like. In fact, he looks like a lead singer for a punk metal band – with tattoos on his arms and neck, his hair styled carefully, and his beard well-trimmed. He is wearing tight jeans and a black button up shirt. He extends his gloved hand, smiling, which gives the whole situation an oddly formal vibe.

"Joe Beringer," he says.

"Royal," I say, making a conscious effort not to share my last name.

He shakes hands with the others, greeting Darryl warmly.

"I understand you have a criminal that I need to pick up?" He says looking around the room.

"Yes, we've moved him to the basement," Darryl answers.

"He's very dangerous, I cannot stress that enough," I add.

"I understand. I've brought tranquilizers for the trip, and restraints."

"Good," Darryl says. "He is more than one man can handle if he is conscious."

"Where did you find him?" Joe asks as we head to the basement.

"We have been tracking him for months trying to find enough proof for a murder conviction," I say.

"I'm guessing there is no proof, if you've asked for our services."

"There was a *situation*, and now we need to get rid of him without a trace."

"Well you have contacted the right person." Joe smiles.

When we enter the basement, August is slumped forward, shirtless and coated in dried blood. He is breathing shallowly, but not moving.

"How long has he been out?"

"About fourteen hours," Darryl estimates.

Joe removes several zip ties from his backpack, along with a syringe full of cloudy liquid. He moves confidently as though he has performed this act millions times. He stabs the needle into the back of August's arm, and pushes the plunger. Then he puts the cap on and tosses it back into his bag.

Next, he attaches the zip ties to August's wrists. With the help of Anthony, he lifts August to his feet, and the two men carry him up the stairs. Outside, in the cool early morning they load August into the black SUV Joe had parked on the dewy lawn.

"That's bullet proof glass separating the criminal from the rest of the vehicle," Joe says proudly. "This vehicle has been modified specifically for our services."

"And we are thankful for your services," I say shaking Joe's hand, and trying to sound grateful.

"Not a problem. It was great meeting you," Joe says in a very businesslike tone.

I watch as he gets into the car and disappears through the mist. I watch knowing that behind the bullet proof glass, there is a monster that I want nothing more than to kill. I will never know the end of the story.

It feels as though a chunk of my life is suddenly missing; like the death of a loved one, or a bad breakup. The vengeance I want for my son's death will never truly be attained.

-PART THREE-
THE BEGINNING

ONE

The pocket watch shimmers in the sunlight, and I wonder why I am allowed to keep it. Everything has been taken from me, apart from this watch and my clothing. My house, my life, and my freedom are no longer available to me – and somehow, I feel perfectly fine about it. I stare at the watch as it ticks on, my breath going in and out. I will likely never know if this watch is on time – I have nothing to compare it to. This fact causes the hair on my neck to stand on end. I wait for hours like this, I wait for something interesting to happen. I have been caught, but not sent to prison – instead, I am forced into some sort of enclosure like an animal. I have barely explored the area, but I am certain there is no shelter for me here, and certainly no modern amenities.

In the early days before the others came, I felt empty; my purpose stripped from me, and my life meaningless. It was all very dramatic and life changing, as you can probably imagine. Or maybe you cannot imagine my perspective – the perspective of someone who kills others for fun and divine purpose. As someone trapped in a lifestyle of the mundane and ordinary – perhaps you can.

To this day, I cannot tell you exactly who created the zoo,and why. I only know that the origin dates back longer than my entire life. It had become a tradition in the Beringer family, one that started in a basement and worked its way up to a well-organized 10 acre project, so isolated the Beringer family never lost sleep over it being discovered. Nobody would challenge them, even if it was discovered.

As a person on the other side of the fence, it took me just under a month to find someone I could gain information from – though I am a little embarrassed to say that it took me so long.

Roger Hampton is one of the twenty fence patrol men that guard the area day and night. I targeted Roger because he is a member of the Beringer family by marriage, and he seems to take pity on me. I also think he is fascinated with me.

"What does it feel like?" He asked me one night during his shift.

I was sitting on a fallen tree, just a few feet from the fence in the darkness. "It feels like life being poured into your body." I smile, remembering the sensation of killing.

Roger swallows and takes a step forward. I have him hooked on my every word, completely absorbed.

"It is everything at once – the power of that feeling is blinding."

He returns almost every night to the same spot, to hear my stories and question my motives. I give him the answers he wants to hear, some of them true, and some not. Before he realizes, Roger is telling me more about his life than he should.

"There will be more people coming in soon," he reveals to me during one of our talks. "Business has been slow lately, but we have some projects on the horizon."

"More like me?" I say curiously.

"Oh yeah, lots of crazies... no offense." He laughs.

"Where do you get them?"

Roger pauses, clearly wondering if he should tell me.

"Well, I guess you can know. I mean, you aren't going anywhere right?" Says Roger.

"Right," I say with gritted teeth.

"We help people catch killers, and we get to keep them." Roger mindlessly taps his fingers against his flashlight holster. "We assure that the killer will be *'taken care of'*, and that justice will be served, and then we bring 'em here, to the zoo."

"And what do you do with them after?" I ask, confused. I was alone at the time.

"What do you mean after? There is no

after!" Roger laughs.

"So everyone dies here?"

"If you put a bunch of dangerous animals together in a cage, they usually kill each other."

I think about it for a moment, it makes a lot of sense. Everyone who is brought to the zoo, will fight, and die in the zoo.

"But what if there is one left?"

"There is always a new shipment. Don't worry, you won't be alone for long."

I try to conceal my excitement, but I am overwhelmed at the prospect of having rivals. The entire idea behind the zoo is perfect. Suddenly, the idea of spending my life behind a fence seems like great fun. Of course, I will never be killed because it is impossible. Instead, I will make the zoo my domain, and reign over it for the rest of my life. Finally, I have a kingdom.

As the months go on, and the *others* come pouring in, I try different methods of removing threats within the enclosure. Eventually I find one I like best. For a while I befriended the others, or tried to seem innocent.

I kept them in the dark, confused about the *whys* and *hows*. Knowledge has kept me above everyone else, and the more time I have spent, the more I learn. I am becoming something of a teacher's pet, though nobody has to teach me to do what I do. Gifts pour in from my supporters in the Beringer family – I am their *superstar*.

I do a lot for them by eliminating the people they send in, and by giving them the entertainment, and pleasure, of watching me do it. At the end of every month when the enclosure has been wiped clean, I am allowed to make a list of the things I require for the next month. Freshly pressed clothes, water, food, almost anything I want is provided for me. It is better than living on the outside – it is my dream come true.

Despite the fact that I can kill freely, and that I am given everything I need, I still lack one thing. My goal is to make the world better, I have an addiction to freeing beautiful, perfect creatures from an imperfect world. Unfortunately, the people sent to the zoo are neither beautiful, nor perfect. Though killing them does give me satisfaction of a sort, my true passion is not being fulfilled.

For several weeks I ponder the issue, and try to find a solution to the problem. All of a sudden, the thought comes to me, and I realize how stupid I am. If I want something, I simply ask, and the Beringer family will provide. It is true, however, that I have never asked for something so large...

"If I asked for a person to be brought here, would my wishes be granted?" I ask Roger during one of our visits.

"A person!? What do you want with a person!?" He says as his face twists in confusion. "We bring in people every month!"

"They are all men," I say calmly.

Roger looks at me for a moment without saying a word, and then he begins to laugh hysterically.

"Oh you want a lady-friend!"

"It's not what you think, I have requirements for my... *hobby*."

"Requirements, eh?" He says pulling out a notepad. "Let me know what you have in mind, and I'll relay the message. I can't make promises though, we have to be careful who we bring in."

"That is understandable."

"We can't be taking innocents, unless the boss OK's it." He reaches for the pen in his breast pocket. "Now then, what can I get ya?"

I feel odd, like I'm ordering at a drive-through restaurant.

"I need someone perfect. Beautiful."

"And?"

"That's all."

"That's kind of shallow, don't you think?"

"I'm not looking for a wife," I say sharply.

"OK, OK. No preference for race? Hair color? Build?"

"No."

"Alright, so I've got 'a beautiful female'." Roger lets out a raspy laugh – too many years of smoking had done a number on his voice.

I do not reply, I am done talking for the night. As I walk away he shouts over the fence.

"No promises!"

I know perfectly well that I can survive without my request, but I also know how much sweeter my life could be.

I keep up my usual routine for months, switching between techniques, learning the best ways to kill both quickly, and slowly. I discover the best ways to gain trust and manipulate other killers.

I never lose myself, however, which is extremely important to me. I keep my appearance sharp, well dressed and well groomed. I have no shower, so I improvise by using the stream near my camp. I am able to shave, cut my hair, and polish my shoes, thanks to the kind gifts provided by the Beringer's.

It has become quite the challenge keeping my shirts clean in the bloodbath, but I manage. Even when I don't kill the entire group at once, the Beringer family still provides the items I need – this makes me curious about their intentions. *How long will they allow me to continue living in the zoo, if I am not killing? If I am not being the entertainer, then what am I?*

Roger had informed me that the enclosure was for the purpose of both experimentation, and the punishment of serial killers like myself.

But I would hardly call the zoo a punishment for my life of woes.

I must conclude that the experimentation factor is the only reason I am allowed to remain, and perhaps some crude fascination the family has with me. This would not be the first time that someone found me irresistibly interesting.

On the night before my life changed, I was lying in bed thinking about the day, when I remembered something that put doubt in my mind about getting my prize. The pocket watch I had been given on arrival was sitting inside my pants pocket, pressing against my thigh. It was a reminder that I would not be given everything I wanted. Countless times I had asked for the time of day – both in my formal monthly request, and casually when speaking with Roger.

But I was always denied, never allowed to check the time of my watch against the actual time. More than once I had tried to guess the time based on the sun's position, but it was impossible to get an accurate guess.

It seems odd that the Beringer's would

keep such an infinitesimal detail from me, but perhaps they are testing my mental state. There were times in my youth when I had been tested for much the same thing. My parents thought that I was odd in the head before I learned to hide those parts of myself.

Of course, now I am more than capable of pretending to be normal, but still the pocket watch aches my insides. The watch is my only comfort, and my only torment. I will never let *them* know this, however. It has always been a priority to maintain my appearance, and here, in the zoo, it is no different. I will always conduct myself as a proper human being. I will dress well, and I will have civil conversations with everyone I come into contact with, but this is not the real me.

In the morning, almost as soon as my eyes open, the siren begins to sound. I sit up, a jolt of excitement running through me. *Perhaps my wish has been granted, and she is waiting for me.*

I dress swiftly in my nicest white shirt, and

arm myself with a hunting knife. This knife is all I need to take down the average criminal. Running through the trees, I try to remain light on my feet, practicing the art surprise.

As the excitement and anticipation builds, I start to feel an old familiar sensation. This state of being only comes when I am acting out my purpose in life.

It feels like there is a thread in my mind wrapped tightly around a spool – it keeps me calm and keeps the facade of normalcy in place. But at times like these, I can feel that spool begin to unravel; my mind flowing into its natural, untamed state. I weave in and out of the trees as comfortably as an eagle in the sky. My eyes are facing forward to the spot where I hope my angel is waiting for me.

I do not stop when I pass the tree line, instead, I push forward to the crates where their unconscious bodies lie. My vision turns red when I see that one of the bodies is smaller, more feminine. Her hair is sprayed across her face in a way that makes it impossible to see her properly from my position. She is motionless.

I eliminate the four others with my knife before they have the chance to wake up. A quick throat-slashing does the trick. I don't care about playing games with them now.

They are all men, and all with the same dull faces I see every month when newcomers arrive. They are never unique.

Finally, I draw near to the angel. As I push her blond hair away from her face, I am shocked. This girl is no angel at all; she is average, typical, and completely without mystery. I drop my hand immediately and step back in horror. My excitement is promptly replaced with anger. I let out a scream so feral and wild that it surprises even me. Rarely do I lose control of my temper.

The girl stirs, and I move to her before she can gather the strength to sit up. Her eyes widen as I hover over her, my face inches from hers.

"Go into the woods and hide, stay away from me, and from everyone or you will be dead. This is the last time I will warn you. If I see you again, I'll kill you myself."

The girl is shaking with fear. It is obvious

that she has no idea where she is, or who I am. I turn then, and walk away without looking back.

I feel sick inside, what a terrible trick they have played on me. In this moment, I can feel the punishment that the zoo, by all accounts, should be giving me. I had asked for something so simple and they had raised my hopes beyond the skies.

For several weeks after, I stay hidden in my forest home. Even on those days where I would have had my talks with Roger, I remain in seclusion. I consider breaking out to kill the entire Beringer family one by one – it is certainly a fun fantasy to entertain.

From my home, I can hear an odd whistling sound from the west. The sound bounces off the trees and echoes around me. I ignore it, though it is clear Roger is the source of the sound. He is trying to get my attention, no doubt to ask me about the girl. As the sound persists, I feel increasingly annoyed, and decide to go check it out.

I am not surprised to see Roger sitting by the fence, his face concerned. He stands when I appear.

"I haven't seen you lately. Have you been enjoying your gift?" He says sheepishly. I know they have cameras hidden in the forest, so he already knows my answer.

"Must we really play dumb?" I say through gritted teeth. The conversation has barely started and I am already tired of it.

Roger stares at me in shock, as though he did not expect my reaction to be so up front.

"Is the girl not what you expected?" He says, his voice steady but his hands shaking.

I feel a tremendous sense of satisfaction welling up inside of me. I am able to intimidate him, even from the other side of an electric fence.

"I asked for someone beautiful, *perfect* in appearance. That is all I asked for."

"She is a pretty girl, and we didn't have much to choose from. We had to go inside the family to get her."

"Inside the family?" I say a little surprised.

"Yes, Mr. Barringer offered up his youngest cousin, just to keep you happy. He is pretty invested in you at this point."

"Oh really? And why is that?"

"You are making him money... that's why."

I think about this new information while Roger sits back down on the tree stump.

"Are they broadcasting the security camera's? Or are they streaming it online?" I ask.

"No, it's not that. It is too dangerous for the family to get caught broadcasting something like that. They are allowing people to come in and watch though, it is like a movie theater."

"How are they keeping them quiet?"

"They have to sign a lot of paperwork, legal stuff, you know. Mr. Beringer is very careful about keeping things quiet."

"Of course, this is beyond family tradition now, he's making money."

"And you are the star of the show."

I can't help but feel a burst of pleasure at that. I deserve to be the star after all the hard work I have put into maintaining my position of power.

"So naturally, Mr. Beringer sent me out here to see what we could do about the girl situation. He wants to keep you as comfortable, and happy with your environment as possible."

"Then find me someone more suitable," I say with a grin. "All I ask for is beauty."

Roger sighs, getting to his feet again. "I will pass your message along."

"Good, and inform Mr. Beringer that if he fails to provide me a suitable female, I will be very *disappointed.*"

"Yes, of course."

Roger disappears into the forest, back down the trail that must lead to their headquarters. I sit by the fence for several minutes, thinking everything over. I am so pleased by the news of my star status that I have forgotten all anger I had toward the girl.

Now that I am aware of my position, I can use it to get what I want. I can push even further than before. The zoo has turned into something so much greater than an experimental prison; it is a five star hotel for serial killers, or at least for *this* serial killer.

I think back to my life on the outside, all of the struggles of hiding who I was, while trying to live out my goals and my destiny. There is someone who makes my stay in the zoo a bitter-sweet one, however, and that person is Royal O'Conner.

Royal is a man I had vastly underestimated, and not only that, I had forgotten him entirely. After I murdered his son, I had assumed nobody knew of my involvement – when I killed, nobody ever knew. Nothing in the past had ever been traced back to me like this one. There is no way that Royal knew his actions would lead me to this wonderful place – this sanctuary, where I can continue to do the very things he longs to punish me for.

And yet, even though his obsession with vengeance lead me here, I still feel the need to get back at him for capturing me. I would gladly trade my so-called freedom for this place, it is more of a home to me than anywhere, but I cannot get Royal out of my mind.

I want him dead for being clever enough to discover me. In the outside world, he is the only person alive who has seen what I am and lived. I cannot allow him to continue with that knowledge.

Of course, in the position I hold over the Beringer family, I could simply ask them to take care of Royal for me, but that's no fun. And then a plan formed in my mind with such zeal that I had a difficult time slowing my brain enough to work through the details. Roger had mentioned the girl sent in for me was Mr. Beringer's cousin, meaning they will likely come in and take her out now that I have openly rejected her. Perhaps I can use that moment to make my escape, it would be a bold, and impulsive decision, but it would certainly liven things up.

As the night goes on, I find myself obsessed with the idea of escaping, but there are hurdles that need to be jumped, some that seem impossible. The biggest of those hurdles being the *when* and *where* the family would come for the girl.

If I were to use that moment as my escape, I would need to know the exact time and location where they would enter the enclosure. Then it occurs to me that they may never extract her at all. Perhaps watching her fight for survival amongst dangerous criminals is something the audience wants to see.

The only other option is that they still value her life. If this is true, I can use it to force them into taking her back. If she means anything at all to her cousin, then he would have to come in and take her out if the situation becomes too dire. Maybe she herself is involved in it, under the promise that she will not be harmed.

The days come and go much slower than usual during the next few weeks in the zoo. It gives me time to think on my escape, perhaps too much time. I am beginning to dwell on the details with such intensity that my mind can focus on nothing else.

The girl is no threat to me. She is alone in the forest with no weapons. The sirens have not sounded since her arrival. There is nothing in my entire world that can harm me. I am the top of the food chain. I wait with itching anticipation for the day when I meet with

Roger. Surely he will have some news about my upcoming gift, and then I can push him for more information.

I arrive at the fence well before our typical meeting time. I check the silver pocket watch quickly, and then stow it back inside my pants pocket. I feel calm knowing it's there. Finally, I hear movement in the forest, and Roger emerges looking tired.

"Hello, and good afternoon," he says sitting down on the tree stump with a grunt.

"What news from the Beringer's?" I ask slowly.

"We found a girl for you. But she is quite a handful."

"Oh?"

"We killed two birds with this stone. She's a beauty – well above the girls you see around here."

"What is the other bird?" I ask.

"Well you might not believe this, but she's a criminal, a bad one." He chuckles scratching his bald spot. I raise an eyebrow, but I do not press the matter.

"She's quite young as well."

"How young?" I ask, my heart picking up speed.

"Seventeen. Just graduated high-school. Been on a killin' streak from what we know."

"Ah, *seventeen.*" My interest switches suddenly from my escape plan to my present.

"We are still in the process of capturing her. She's smart, but Joe says he'll have her soon."

Joe is the family's go-to criminal hunter.

"Good. Will you be taking back the other girl?" I ask conversationally.

"Not just yet. Mr. Beringer wants to see where things go for a while. If it gets too hairy in there, we'll come get her."

This is precisely what I want to hear. My heart is soaring with delight – I am getting everything I want, it is too good to be true.

"I understand. I hope Mr. Beringer knows that I will not be held responsible for keeping her alive."

"Oh, well you *are* a serial killer aren't you? You don't expect him to trust you!" Roger says laughing.

"An argument I cannot find fault in," I

say, my mood getting lighter by the minute.

"I hope you will be satisfied with the new girl, we've put in a lot of effort for her. She is certainly one of a kind. You don't get many female serial killers, not to mention *teenage* female serial killers."

"A unique case, certainly," I say shifting in my seat as I think of what she might look like. "I look forward to meeting her."

-PART FOUR-
THE ZOO

ONE

I wake up in a cold, dark room. My hands brush against the ground, and discover a cement floor. I am on my hands and knees, feeling around in the pitch darkness – searching for meaning. *Where am I? How did I get here? Who has taken me?* I am reminded of a party last year when I had drunk myself into a stupor, only to wake up in an unknown location, covered in glitter. I scoot further across the room, probing for clues. I am definitely inside a building, there is no wind and the air smells like mold. My hand bumps into something wet, *water?* No, the texture is thick, *blood?* Maybe. I crawl until I meet the wall and pull myself up. It feels like the wall is also cement; *am I in a basement?* I begin to walk slowly along the wall in search of a door.

It feels like I walk for a very long time before an explosion of light hits my eyes. The light is so blinding that the resulting pain of it forces me to my knees. I hide my face deep in my hands, trying to block it out, but it seems to come from everywhere.

The pain is so intense that I want to pluck out my eyes and end it, but then it dims. I look up, trying desperately to get a glimpse of who, or what has brought me to this place. My eyes are blurry, I can only make out a shadow that crosses in front of me. I freeze as the shadow stops moving.

Then, suddenly, the figure darts toward me, and though I want to fight, I find my limbs getting weaker until I cannot hold myself up. I fall sideways, slamming the side of my face into the cold cement. Pain spreads across my cheekbone.

"Sleep," a distorted voice murmurs, and I obey because it is my only option.

When I wake again, I am tied down. I lie still for a while with my eyes shut, thinking. I have no idea why I am being held captive, but I know I am certainly a prisoner here. *This must be related to the person who kidnapped Hayley and Joe.* I open my eyes and find a different scene than the basement. I am lying outside on a wooden crate that I am chained to. A massive field of tall grass surrounds me. There are trees on one side of the field, opposite a monumental fence with razor wire at the top.

I try to sit up, but the chains hold me down. Glancing as far behind as I can, I see another box with a person chained there. From this angle, I can see nothing of my companion but a pair of dirty work boots.

"H-hey!" I attempt a yell, but my voice cracks. It feels like I haven't spoken in years. The stranger does not move.

I rest my head back on the crate, and wait. I don't know what exactly I am waiting for, but I know something must happen. There has to be a reason. *Who would chain someone to a crate in the middle of nowhere for no reason?* I start to laugh under my breath when I think about the situation. How hilarious it is that I have spent the last month worrying about being caught and sentenced to death.

I jump as a hand touches my neck. When I look over, I see Joe Beringer standing above me holding a syringe in one hand, and a gun in the other.

"Good morning, Lilith," he says smiling. "Don't move now." Joe taps the gun against my temple and I am frozen.

"What are you doing here?" I say, my mouth dry.

"Oh I knew you'd have plenty of questions." He pokes the syringe into my neck — it stings badly. "I'm afraid you only get answers on my terms."

I am starting to feel very dizzy, but I fight the sensation with all my strength.

"It was you," I whisper, floating slowly into unconsciousness.

Joe laughs loudly. "It *is* me."

Two

Something is tickling my face and I want to scratch it, but my arms are so tired. I am on my stomach this time, still tied to the old crate. I crack one eye open and look sideways to the sky. I jump when I see an eye staring back at me.

Someone is sitting on my back, staring down at me. I can feel a nose touching my cheek – hot breath on my face. When I try to move, more weight presses down on my back.

"You are an angel." The voice is dreamy and beautiful, but dripping with madness.

Suddenly, I am weightless, I am flying through the air and minutes pass before I realize that I am being carried on the shoulder of the stranger.

I stare at his back, curious and exhausted. *Is he wearing a suit?* I stroke the fine charcoal gray material with my pinky finger. The fabric is silky, and oddly comforting. I don't recall how I came to be untied.

"I'm thrilled to finally get my angel," the voice says. "I haven't seen you in months."

I try to remember meeting him in the past, but I don't recall. I lift my head to look at the crates where I had been chained. Four crates are lined up, all of them empty.

"Where am I?"

"The zoo of course." The peculiar man chuckles; amused by my ignorance. "Bring the white rabbit to the zoo!" He shrieks.

"Who are you?" I ask, tiring of his nonsensical chatter.

"August Eaton my darling girl, but you can call me August," he says.

I stay quiet for a while. It is nice that I don't have to walk, but his shoulder pressing into my stomach is getting old.

"Can you put me down?" I ask.

"Nope," he says in a chipper fashion.

"Why not?"

"Because angels fly away," August says.

It seems arguing is pointless. I feel as though I should be afraid, but I am only curious. I know my strength, and I am willing to kill to survive. However, in the moment I am weak and tired. I will deal with this psychopath later, but only when he is done being useful to me. I listen to the man hum happily as he carries me to the forest. I recognize the tune as *Penny Lane – The Beatles? Really?*

"Home is just around the corner," he says patting my bottom.

"Home?"

"Oh yes, you don't think I live in the grass do you? Into the rabbit hole and to the outdoor tea table?" He adjusts me on his shoulder, and I feel a bit more comfortable. "How would I keep the dirt off my shoes?" He falls into a fit of laughter that shakes my entire body. He pauses for a moment to let himself recover, and then continues walking.I am beginning to get annoyed with my limited view, but then we stop.

"Let me just find a nice spot..." he murmurs, spinning me around. Suddenly, I am hoisted onto a bed of leaves with a crunch. For the first time, I get a good look at the insane man.

To my surprise he is gloriously handsome, with bright green eyes and chiseled features. His hair is dark and styled neatly. His suit is tailored perfectly to his body, revealing just enough for me to gather that he is in amazing physical shape. I am stunned by what I see. This man is completely and totally insane, and yet he looks like a wealthy male model.

"You are really something," August says staring at me.

"O-oh?" My voice cracks. He smiles as though he knows exactly what put me into this dumbfounded state.

"You smell like soap and flowers," he says.

"Well that's good to know. I've been out of it for a while, not sure if I've showered..."

"Oh, they took care of all that before you

came in, and if you are *really* good, they let you have treats."

"Who are they? Where am I?"

August pauses, thinking. "What do I get if I tell you?" He grins.

"The pleasure of making me happy," I say, grinning back.

"Well now, that's a good offer." He reaches inside his suit jacket and pulls out a gruesome dagger. It is crooked and rusty, with blood stains on the handle. My heart skips a beat.

"You and I are the same species my little rabbit." He touches the blade with his thumb and forefinger as he steps closer.

I refuse to move away, despite my instincts screaming *RUN*.

"We are animals, and animals need a cage, a zoo if you will."

"So this is some kind of prison?"

August crouches down beside me, his lovely eyes looking right into mine.

"You could call it that, though it's more of an *alternative* to prison."

"Do you kill too?" I ask looking at the blade, and then back up at him sweetly.

"I am, who I am, baby doll."

He lets the dagger drop from his hands, and I hear it hit something on the ground. Looking down over the edge of my makeshift bed, I see my white rabbit mask lying there, August's dagger stabbing through one of the eyes. I know I am hallucinating, but the sight is deeply traumatizing. I feel my heart quicken as I fade into a deep, dreamless sleep.

I don't know how long I am unconscious after that. August is no good with time, and when I ask him about it later, he never gives me the answers I want. He always makes up some riddle, or tries to make a joke of it.

I wake up in a cold sweat, very hungry and very thirsty. I look around and find that I am under a canopy of woven tree limbs, a comfortable breeze touching my skin. I sit up, waiting for August, or Joe, to come back for me, but there is nobody, the place seems totally deserted.

I stand shakily, my whole body is sore and

stiff, as though I've been lying in one spot for months. My rabbit mask is gone. A hefty fallen log blocks off one side of the canopy like a wall. Another side is open, while two more are covered in thick ivy that ripples and sways in the wind. A loud tapping sound makes me jump, I swing around to look at the fallen tree where the sound had come from, but I see nothing.

I walk through the ivy wall, and around to the other side of the tree. When I turn the corner, I am surprised to see a beautiful woodpecker tapping the tree trunk with amazing force. It notices me and flies off, soaring high into the trees above where I lose track of it in the thick branches. I turn to my home in the trees and stare at it for a few moments. *I am in quite a pickle.* For starters, I have no idea where I am, or why. All I have to go on is the word of a psychopath who I'm not sure really exists beyond my imagination.

It all seems like someone is playing a trick on me. I have no supplies to speak of, so taking off in the forest is a gamble, but staying in one spot would provide me no more safety beyond cover from the rain.

I consider that maybe Joe had given me a drug that causes hallucinations. Perhaps he had brought me here to torture and kill, like I'm sure he did with Hayley. Of course, I have no proof he has taken Hayley, but the odds are looking good.

"Oh angel, you are awake!" The voice startles me, and I quickly turn around.

It is August, and it seems he is real after all. He stands before me wearing the same gray suit. He looks freshly shaved, his hair styled perfectly.

"Good morning," I say.

He seems delighted by my response. "You are in a good mood."

"Sleep does that to me."

August steps forward and looks at me carefully. "You do seem well rested enough." His face is concerned.

"Is this your place?" I ask.

"The whole zoo is my place, yes." He laughs. "It's survival of the fittest here, and well, look at me." He poses briefly, flexing his muscles.

"How many others are there?"

"Hmm...one?" He says thinking.

"What? I saw four crates when you carried me away."

"In here you kill to survive, and I've been doing just that." He says sitting down on my bed of twigs.

"You killed them all on your own?"

"Yes. Is that so hard to imagine?" He smiles, making me feel dizzy.

"You just seem so, friendly?"

He laughs loudly. "Thank you."

"So who is left?"

"Besides you and me? Some girl, no idea who she is."

"Not a threat?" I ask.

"Ha, hardly. She screamed and ran as soon as she was free." He straightens his tie. "Most people come in ready for a fight, especially if they know about me."

"How do people get here?"

"It's part of an experiment in entertainment. Criminals are sent here to see how they interact with those like them."

"But I'm not a criminal! I was attacked,

and brought here with no evidence against me." I can feel my heart starting to race.

"Aw, sweetie. You've already confessed."

"What are you talking about?"

"You mean, you don't remember that *'are you a killer too?'* business?"

My mind flashes back to when I was first brought here. I was so heavily drugged that it seems like a dream.

"I was drugged! None of that could possibly stand up in court. Not to mention I haven't even been to court yet. This is i*llegal.*"

"Illegal it may be, but nobody is around to know about it, at least nobody of consequence."

"So, I'm just supposed to accept this?"

"Accepting is your only option."

I sit down on the grass and rest my back against the fallen tree. I can't bring myself to believe that this is all I have left. *There is a way out, and I am going to find it. Maybe once I get free I can head abroad. I am not on any wanted lists, after all...not yet.*

As far as I know, there is no warrant for my arrest. I can simply leave the country once

I am free, and make my own life somewhere safe. Of course, if I am to continue my lifestyle – this hobby of blood – I have to be more cautious. I can't keep leaving the country every time I screw up.

"Who are you, anyway?" I ask.

"I told you, my name is August Eaton."

"I know your name, but *who* are you?"

He pauses for a bit. "I'm a predator. I seek out beauty and innocence, and then I set it free," he says making a dramatic hand motion with the word 'free'. He looks even more insane than before.

"You don't set it free, you destroy it. That's what *we* do."

"I had hoped you would understand..." August says sadly.

"I understand perfectly. I understand more than most."

He looks at me with a blank, almost goofy stare. I find it hard to imagine that he is dangerous, but if he has killed everyone here, he must be.

"What do you feel like? When you kill someone?" I ask.

He sits up a little straighter; it seems that he loves this topic.

"I feel intensely alive. I feel like I'm doing what I should, and that I'm making the world better... making myself better."

"I do it for the fun," I say smiling. "I'm a predator too, though most people think I'm the prey."

He laughs again. "I see the blood-lust in your eyes. You are a different kind of angel."

"I'm not an angel. I'm a fox dressed as a little white rabbit. I steal lives from people without remorse."

"This is just the place for you, then." He turns serious suddenly. "We are allowed, and even encouraged to kill here. It may seem like being trapped in this box means we are confined somehow, but in reality, we are free here."

"We are in danger here," I say.

He grins widely; his teeth straight and perfect.

"You are in no danger here, my angel, if you stay with me, that is." His words are laced in poison, a threat lying just under the surface.

It is as though *he* would be the one to kill me if I left. I smile back at him sweetly.

"Why would I leave? What do I have to gain elsewhere?"

"You play a smart game. Keep it up." He stands then, and walks over to me, holding out his hand. "Now, let me show you the rest of my home."

I raise my eyebrow, I had thought the cozy canopy was his home. He lifts me up to face him, placing his hands on my shoulders.

"How do you feel?" He asks, his eyes shining, beautifully reflecting the green of the forest.

"A little tired, but good."

"Good," he says releasing my shoulders and taking my hand.

We walk through the trees for at least five minutes before we stop. I look around confused; there is no home here at all, only empty forest.

"Where is it?" I ask.

"Up," he says simply.

I look up, and to my surprise, there is an enormous tree house intricately woven through the tops of the timber. It is made from the same branches of the canopy room, but far more elaborate.

"I like to sleep above ground, gives me an advantage."

"It's amazing," I say, awestruck.

"Wait until you see it from up there."

August leads me up the hand-made ladder, to the tree house at the top. When he pulls me up, the first thing I see is the amazing view. From the heights I can see beyond the trees – and beyond the fence that keeps us confined. Open land goes on for miles, I can even see mountains in the distance. More than anything, this view reveals how very far from home I must be. The terrain is unlike anything I have seen in person. This place is wild, beautiful, and isolated.

"Wow," I say out loud, taking in the outlook – I want to stare at it forever.

"Like a dream," he says in agreement. "This is where I spend my days."

I glance around the tree house and see that it is quite cozy. Everything is hand-made, and made well. I don't know how August has made some of it on his own. I feel a little impressed by his crafting skills. A cracked mirror sits in the corner, a large piece of glass is missing.

"Where did you get that?" I ask.

"It was a gift." He seems shy suddenly. "I don't want to forget myself while I'm in here."

"A gift from who?"

"The people who own this place." I walk to the other side of the room and see a small bed that has been crafted from foliage and clothing – It looks very comfortable.

"Of course, you can share my comforts, if you like. An angel shouldn't sleep on the ground," says August.

I laugh despite my discomfort. "I'm happy with the bed you made for me."

He seems let down, but happy that I like his work. "Good, I was worried. I didn't have much time..." His hand twitches.

"That's perfectly understandable. I guess you weren't expecting guests."

"No," he says sadly.

"Why are you keeping me alive?" I ask bluntly. He seems taken aback by the question and shifts nervously. "You can tell me," I add.

"I hadn't seen an angel for a long time, and when I saw you, I wanted to set you free – but I am greedy." August stares at the floor.

"Set me free?"

"That's what I do. I find angels, and I let their blood out, so they can be free."

I feel my heartbeat quicken. *This man is going to kill me. Though he hasn't killed me yet, I'm certain he will try.*

"You don't want to be alone, I don't think that's greedy."

He looks at me with an unreadable expression, and then looks out over the treetops.

"You can stay as long as you want," he says sincerely, "I understand it won't last forever."

I'm not sure if he means my life, or our living arrangements, but either way he is right; neither will last forever. We are quiet for a while, watching the light of the day fade. My stomach growls loudly and August chuckles.

"Hungry?" He asks.

"A bit."

August crosses the room, crouching down

next to a bag that appears to have been crafted from an old shirt. He pulls out a handful of berries, and hands them to me.

"I picked them yesterday, you are just in time."

"Thank you," I say taking them. "What do you do in the winter?" I ask.

August laughs. "I don't live on berries, if that's what you think. I get plenty of supplies from the people in charge. I've planted potatoes and carrots. I hunt when I can, and fish in the streams." He sits down next to me, leaning against the wall of the tree house.

"You have quite a life here," I say popping a berry into my mouth – it is sweet and tangy.

"It beats the alternative, I suppose."

We talk for hours while the sun sets – *What a beautiful place to watch the land grow dark.* I begin to feel tired suddenly, and decide to retreat to my bed on the ground. August grabs my arm when I stand, he already knows what I am going to say.

"I know you won't stay with me." Something in his expression is comforting, and

I feel bad leaving him.

"You are correct."

"If you need anything, I'll be listening," he says touching my chin. "Goodnight, my angel."

"Goodnight." I turn quickly, bewildered by my conflicting emotions.

This man is obviously ill, but what am I? We are both on the same level – we both kill for reasons that are not justifiable. I am attracted to him in more ways than one, but I am also aware that he can take my life any time he pleases. I don't know him, but I feel the similarities between us.

I follow the trail back to my bed and fall down with a soft crunch on the leaves. I have to be ready for anything; I am alone with a murderer who intends to take my life. I cannot trust him, but I have to stay with him. For some reason he has decided I should live, and I have to figure out what that reason is. I have to make myself a *priority* to him.

The question is, does August Eaton have any sense of attachment? I think back to my box of letters floating away in the sea, and the first time I was told of Hayley's disappearance

– I felt nothing, no attachment held me to those things.

If that is the common trait that allows people like August and myself to kill without remorse, than maybe he feels the same about me. Perhaps he can never grow attached to me, at least not in a way that would prevent my death at his hands.

I stay up half the night thinking. I know very little about where I am, or why. Though I hardly care what has happened to Hayley, I can't help but wonder why they had taken her, or if they had taken her at all.

Maybe her disappearance is simply a coincidence that has no relation to my capture – it seems too strange that both should happen at once.

And then there is Joe's involvement. How could he be a part of something like this and just stumble upon someone like me at a party. *What kind of luck would permit an event like that? Who would even suspect me of committing a crime like murder? As far as I know, I have my bases covered.*

As my thoughts jumble into one another,

my mind drifts slowly until I fall asleep with the breeze caressing my face.

THREE

The siren sounding wakes me from a deep sleep. My last memory is convincing August to let me sleep in the canopy. I know what he wants from me, and I am not about to give it in to him. *I am nobody's prey.* I sometimes use promises of love, a smile, or a kiss, to lure someone into thinking I am prey to be caught, and then I would, in turn, prey on them.

I shoot out of bed, the siren wailing again. I run for the tree house, knowing that whatever the siren signifies, I am better off with someone who knows the ropes. I had run only a few feet when I nearly run face first into August.

He is shirtless and holding a large piece of glass in his hand. The glass is bound at the bottom with leather for a handle. His ivory skin glows in the moonlight, and when he speaks to me his teeth appear to glow as well.

"We have new friends to deal with." He is jubilant.

"New killers?"

"Yes, so soon too... do you feel up for a run?"

"You mean, chase them down?" I ask.

"Yes." His eyes are glowing with excitement, and I begin to feel excited too.

He grabs my hand and leads me to the edge of the forest, the same path he used to bring me here.

We stop at the edge of the trees, and look toward the far end of the field. Flashlights move back and forth, the silhouettes of two people move amongst large black shapes, they look like the crates where I had been tied before.

"We wait for a few minutes before we make a move," he says in a whisper.

The flashlights disappear, the shapes in the distance do not move. The wind pushes the tall grass back and forth intermittently, and my heart races.

I am excited at the prospect of killing freely for the first time. Not to mention, sharing the joy of the experience with someone else – someone who understands the way it feels; the euphoria. When I was younger, before I began acting out my fantasies, I would daydream about hunting whenever I wanted, out in the open and without judgment. Of course, I knew this was an idle fantasy at the time, I would have never expected my dreams would turn into reality.

If August is telling the truth, and we really are encouraged to kill in this place, then why would I ever want to leave? Perhaps it's ingrained in all creatures – the need to be free. When you have everything you want, but at the cost of your freedom, it makes you reconsider what you value most. *Is it freedom?*

Or something else that I crave most?

August pulls me into the tall grass, where we crouch down, walking slowly to the place where the newcomers will be coming out of their stupor.

He stops abruptly and turns to me. August reaches down at his side in the darkness and takes out a large hunting knife, handing it to me with a smirk.

"Where did you get this?" I say in a hushed tone.

"It was a gift. I told you, if you behave, you get treats." I take the blade and touch the edge, it is razor sharp. The blade is at least ten inches, long enough to do serious damage.

August moves forward again and I follow closely behind him. Without warning, he hurtles forward and I try with all my strength to keep up, but he is incredibly fast.

He leaps on top of a man who has just opened his eyes. He is a rough-looking middle-aged man, with thinning gray hair and a pot belly. His arms are covered in faded tattoos, and a thin scar runs the length of his face.

"You reek of beer," August says angrily.

"You are filthy! What do you think this is?" August grabs the man's face and looks him in the eyes. The man looks back, clearly afraid.

"Who-who are you?"

"That's what they all ask. Could you try for some originality? We don't have much time to get to know each other. You want to make a good impression, don't you?" August laughs maniacally.

The man yells and swings at August who dodges without a second thought. Before the man can prepare another blow, August thrusts his glass blade in the man's neck. He twitches and makes a disgusting gurgling sound. Blood pours out over one of the old crates, staining it black in the dim light.

"You get that one!" August shouts, pointing at another body on the crate near me. The stranger is lying on his stomach, in the same position I was when I woke up here.

I run over to the crate and see a man, he is very old and barely breathing. I touch his cheek, and his eyes fly open. He doesn't say a word to me, but he looks as though he knows exactly what is going to happen.

"This is the end, I'm afraid," I say, not aggressively, but tenderly. The old man looks at me with relief.

"I've been waiting so long for this," he says peacefully. "I'm ready." He closes his eyes and waits.

I lift my knife and lay it on his throat, but I can't strike. Something is wrong with me, there is a lump in the back of my throat. *Am I nervous?* August emerges and thrusts his blade quickly into the old man's neck.

He glances at me strangely, and then moves on to the last man of the group. When all of them lie dead, August picks through their clothing for anything useful. He takes their belts, shoes, and the occasional items of clothing. It is interesting to watch him work.

"Why don't you let them speak first, what if they are on your side?" I ask.

"I can see their souls. None of them would be a friend in here."

I am afraid to ask what he means by "see their souls". I am aware that August is unstable, and psychotic, but I would like to pretend he is normal for the sake of my own sanity.

"What about the girl you let free? Did you see her soul?" I ask.

"She is inconsequential. She was no harm to me, and I gained nothing by killing her." His logic seems solid for once.

"Where do you think she is?"

"Hiding in the woods, maybe dead if she didn't find water."

I follow August back to our home in the woods. Even though I have just arrived, it feels like home to me – or at least more of a home than I have ever had. I am comfortable, and safe for the time being. My biggest threat is the man who provides this safety. For now I am at peace with the situation.

"We can use these supplies to help secure the tree house," he says, hoisting the pile onto my bed. "If you intend on staying here, we can build a wall on this side for more security," he says, walking over to the wall of vines blowing in the wind.

"It seems to be getting colder. I wouldn't mind some more protection from the elements."

"If you would just stay in the tree house, it would be much safer," he says looking at me seriously.

I don't want to make him angry, but I don't want to stay in the tree house either.

"If you make me a separate bed, I'll stay in the tree house." I say compromising. He considers this for a minute.

"I can move most of this bed up to the tree house easily enough. And with the stock of clothing I've collected, we can make it more comfortable." He seems happier about this arrangement than I anticipated.

"I can help. I'm not *totally* useless, you know."

He laughs. "Good. Sling a few of those supplies over your shoulder, and head up to the tree house then," August says, picking up his own burden.

The two of us manage to get all of the necessary items up the ladder easily. I help in any way I can as August prepares a space for me.

Part of me feels that being this close to him is dangerous, but at the same time, I have no other options. I need to keep him at least partially satisfied.

The Next day, while August works on reinforcing the stability of our treetop home, I decide to take a stroll around the area and explore.

When I leave, August seems wary but allows me to go without arguing. It is obvious that even if I do run away, he can easily find me.

There is only one trail and it leads back to the canopy and out of the forest, so I move in the opposite direction. The pine trees make the walk easy – the fallen needles work well to prevent plant life from overtaking the spaces between the tree trunks. I have nothing to fear here, I can do and be whatever I want. The feeling is tremendous.

I enjoy the walk alone, knowing that I have nowhere to be and nothing to do. Eventually, the trickling sound of running water meets my ears amongst the chirping birds. The trees thin and a small stream comes into view, it is lined with rocks on both sides, and flowing peacefully downhill and into the forest, until I can no longer see it.

I crouch down at the edge, and stick my fingers into the clear water. It is cold, and appears clean. Small fish come up to my fingers and investigate after a few minutes; I hold my hands still and watch them. I sit by the stream for a very long time, watching the water, and the trees, and the life of the forest around me. It is such a beautiful sight.

When the sun is halfway up, I decide to make my way back. It is a straight line from the stream to the tree house. Obviously August had planned the placement of the tree house to be directly between the stream and the field.

My mind wanders to the fence I had seen along the field of waving grass. I assume the giant barrier, with its wire top, is meant to keep us in, but I have not inspected it for myself yet. When I arrive back at the tree house, August is working on the ladder.

"Welcome back," he says keeping his eyes on his work. He is securing the ladder with the shoelaces he had taken from one of the men.

"I found the stream. It's lovely."

"Ah, yes. Perfect for trapping fish as well."

"I didn't see a fence in that direction." I lean against the other side of the ladder and watch his progress.

"That's because the fence is much further away on the other side. It reaches far behind the trees, to the west, and then beyond the river. It's only visible from the field, where the trees are scarce."

"It seems kind of minuscule."

"What do you mean?"

"It just seems kind of a pathetic attempt to keep people like you and I from escaping."

"Well it happens to be electrified. The perimeter is also guarded securely," August says, wiping his hands on a piece of cloth.

He is dressed tidy as ever, though he has abandoned his suit jacket, wearing only a white button down shirt, gray slacks, and shiny black shoes.

"Still, not impossible to escape," I say.

"Why would we escape?" He says laughing. "What is out there for us but prison, or death?"

I know he is right, of course, but I still feel

anxious. Being forced to linger anywhere makes me feel claustrophobic. And surely they will not leave us here forever. If this is some kind of experiment, eventually it will have to end.

When it does, we will likely be killed, or sent off to prison. I do not mention any of my insecurities to August. Staying on the same page will make him feel secure, and possibly keep me alive longer.

"You are right," I say smiling. I touch the ladder where he has been working. "This looks great."

"I'm just doing a bit of upkeep. Now that I have you here I want everything nice, angels need nice things," he says.

"You know, you never asked my name," I say.

"Does it matter? Angels like you should be called what you are."

"Aren't you curious?"

"Why would I be curious?" He looks utterly dumbfounded.

"Never mind," I say. "It's not important."

"I've prepared some fish fillets for dinner

tonight. While you were gone, I got the fire pit ready."

"You have a fire pit?" I say, surprised. I had assumed we would be cooking everything over a shabby camp fire, if even that.

"I have been here for a long time," says August, chuckling. He seems to find me endlessly entertaining.

Later that night by the fire, we eat fish and enjoy the cool weather. Despite his moments of insanity, I find August to be wonderful company. He is considerate, and listens to every word I say. In almost every sense, he is the perfect man. Other times, he leaves me wondering about my safety.

"This *zoo...* do you know much about why it's here?" I ask as August puts another fillet on the fire.

"I only know what I've observed over the time I've spent here. They try to keep everything very secretive, but it's easy to see past their fences, and hear what they think I cannot."

"What have you heard?" I ask.

"Whispers of experimentation, something kept secret from the authorities. If I were to guess, this whole thing is privately run."

"By who?"

"It's not important." He touches my chin for a second, and then stokes the fire with his hunting knife.

"Aren't you curious about all of this? Don't you want to know who is keeping us here, and for what purpose?"

"Not at all," he says seriously. "My life has been improved by being here."

"Well, I want to find out. I can't just stay here in the dark without knowing." His facial expression changes, he is disappointed.

"And what will you do when you know? What better place is there for you... for me?"

I want so badly to form the perfect answer, to prove to him that I am right – instead, I lean forward and I kiss him.

I cannot tell you why I made this move, or if I even wanted the kiss. When we part he seems happy, but just as bewildered as I am.

"If I'm satisfied with being here – if I'm

satisfied with anything, the game is over," I say truthfully. "The adventure, the mystery, it will all be over." I look into the flames as I speak, wondering if my words reach him.

I see August from the corner of my eye as he stands, and walks behind me. A million scenarios form in my mind before I see him on the opposite side moving toward the trees. I stay in my seat for a long time, looking into the eyes of the fire pit, the roaring energy is a soul that understands me.

I do not call to August, nor do I question where he is going in the darkness. I know that we need this moment to ourselves. The kiss was a last minute decision, one I hadn't thought through, and that makes it dangerous. Something as simple as a kiss can bring me harm when it involves someone as unstable as August.

For the rest of the night I don't see him. The night moves quickly to days, and after a week has passed, I am both hopeful and worried. Alone, my chances of survival drop, but how great are the chances of August killing me himself?

I wait every night for another delivery of killers, and my only comfort is in the little knowledge I have of this place. This is the one advantage I have, the single fact that I am aware of something that others are not.

The morning dawns through the cracks of a storm cloud. I hold my breath until the next roll of thunder. Lying alone in the tree house, staring at the weathered wood, I let my mind go blank. The thunder slams the forest and I inhale, the smell of fresh rain flooding my nose and lungs.

Suddenly, a scream throws my heart into a fit. I stand up, instantly prepared to defend myself. My hand wraps around my knife as another scream fills the tree house. I hurry to the glassless window and look down to the clearing, taking care to keep myself concealed.

At first, I see nothing, but as my eyes dart around the base of the tree house, a girl appears stumbling through the bushes. She falls and turns to look behind her, letting out another scream and scrambling to her feet. It is clear that she is being pursued, and I take a second to decide if interfering is in my best interest.

I did not hear the trumpet signaling new arrivals, had the storm masked it? My interest is peaked when a man hustles after the girl. He is short, bulky, and dirty. His thick, hairy arms grip what appears to be a heavy tree limb. The girl runs under the tree house, not noticing it. The hulking man follows, I catch a glimpse of his bald spot as he runs after her.

In this instant, I decide to do something daring. I sprint across the room to the opposite window and climb over the edge – waiting for the perfect moment.

First, I see the girl, then just as the man appears, I let out a feral scream that stops him in his tracks. The man looks up, startled as I dive down on him with my knife aimed carefully.

The impact sends us both flying to the ground. A sudden pain in my arm causes me to lose grip on my knife. My head slams into a tree trunk, dazed, I look around for the attacker. Through my blurred vision I see a large figure on the ground, twitching. I look down and see a large scratch on my arm, nothing fatal.

I get up feeling a little wobbly, and move to where my victim fell. The man is clutching his thick neck, blood pouring between his fingers. I spot the handle of my knife sticking up between his neck and shoulder. Grabbing the handle, I twist and slash it out to finish the job. The man gurgles and then falls silent.

Wiping my knife on my light blue t-shirt, I look around for the girl, but I don't see her anywhere in the clearing around the tree house. There is no point in chasing after her, or shouting my alliance through the trees. For all I know, the girl could be my enemy, and if I haven't earned her trust by saving her life, nothing I can say will.

I leave the body, and head for the drop off zone. It takes several minutes to reach the clearing near the fence, and as soon as I arrive, I see something unusual.

There are no crates, empty or inhabited. No criminals are strapped down anywhere.

Instead, I count eight people leaving through the fence dressed in all black tactical gear. They are holding what appears to be guns of some kind, and in between two of them is a grungy-looking man bound by handcuffs, being toted beyond the fence.

I lean back into the trees and watch as the gate closes and the electric fence buzzes to life. I see movement just beyond the fence, the people in black are moving through the trees as though they are searching for something. I am hit with the realization that they could be searching for the girl I had seen earlier. It appears as though they are removing some of the criminals from the enclosure. *Is August among them?*

Hurrying back to the tree house, I keep my eyes open and my knife ready for anything that might be waiting for me. And there is someone waiting for me, but it is not the girl, or the people dressed in black.

To my surprise, August is standing alone in the clearing. He is staring right at me as though he had waited in that spot, knowing exactly where and when I would appear.

"August," I say his name without meaning to as I walk forward to meet him.

He is bloodied, and his clothes are torn. Suddenly, there is a rustling in the trees behind us, we both turn and I glimpse a girl peeking through the trees.

I am stunned into shock by the person I see the moment before she runs away. August stands and starts for her, but I grab his arm.

"I know her," I whisper.

He looks confused. "That's the girl I let go free," says August.

We both run into the woods then, chasing after her. I see something moving ahead and run harder. She comes into view wearing a blue hoodie and jeans, she is running as fast as she can to avoid us. I recognize the hoodie from earlier, she is the girl I saved. I have no time to ponder the situation as she runs faster.

"Wait!" I yell into the trees, but she does not stop.

August passes me, outrunning me and gaining on the girl. Suddenly, she trips on a fallen branch and collapses to the ground. August stops dead in his tracks. When I catch up with him I am shocked to see Hayley lying on her back with a gun pointed right at August's face.

FOUR

"Stop!" I plead. Hayley seems not to notice me, her eyes stay focused on August. "Please, look at me, Hayley!" I say louder.

Her eyes turn to me then and several seconds pass before she recognizes me.

"Lily?" She says, her eyes filling with tears.

"It's me, Hayley. Put the gun down, this is August, he's my friend," I urge her.

She eyes us both suspiciously, the gun shaking in her hands. "He wants to kill me," she says softly.

"I only told you that to keep you away from danger," says August with his silky voice. "Now put my gun down."

I look at him confused. *His gun?*

Hayley looks back and forth between us, trying to decide what to do. "Please just put the gun down, you are safer with us than on your own here," I say.

Slowly, she lowers the weapon to the ground. I approach her, holding my hand out to help her up.

"Give me the gun," I say, and she turns it over in her hand once before handing it to me. She gazes over my shoulder at August, who has not moved an inch.

"You know him?" She asks, wiping the mud off her cheek.

"He has been keeping me safe since I arrived here."

"But he *killed* the others, he killed them all!" She sobs, taking a step back.

"That's what you have to do here to survive, please understand."

Hayley looks away into the forest sniffling. I hand the gun to August.

"What do we do? Why are we here? How do we get out!?" She chokes on another sob.

I glance at August trying to determine what exactly we should say to her, and what information we should withhold.

"This is an experimental facility. A social experiment if you will," says August confidently.

"Like a reality TV show?"

"Yes, but without the television."

"I don't understand," says Hayley, wiping her nose.

"This experiment is purely for the entertainment of the owners, and their select in-house audience. They watch us, they introduce new players, and they see how long we survive – how we interact with each other."

"How long have you been here?" Hayley asks.

"Months, maybe years," he says.

Hayley lets loose a waterfall of fresh tears, and covers her face with her hands. I can't help but roll my eyes at the sheer drama of the situation.

I look at August and see that his face is

serious, and convincingly sincere.

"All we can do right now is stay together, and stay alive," I say, placing my hand on her shoulder with my best imitation of a comforting friend.

"Come back to camp with us, we can make an extra bed," he says in a voice smooth and reassuring. I am impressed by his acting abilities.

We lead her back to the camp without another word. It seems she is too emotional to ask any more questions, which gives us more time to figure out what we will tell her, and what we will do with her.

August tucks her into my old canopy, and brushes the hair out of her face in a fatherly manner. She buries her face in the foliage and sobs.

"We are safe for now, there is nobody in here apart from the three of us," August whispers to her. "Stay here and rest," he orders, and then turns to me.

"Come with me please." August motions for me, and I follow him down the path to the tree house.

I notice the man I killed is gone, and I wonder who, or what, removes the bodies. August does not speak until we reach the top of the tree house. "How attached are you to this girl?" He asks turning to face me.

"I hate her with my entire being. But, she has never caused me harm."

"So I'm assuming that killing her would be against your wishes?"

"Yes."

He sighs deeply, closing his eyes and running his hands over his eyelids softly. "I was afraid of that."

"She is the one you left alive right? Why do you want to kill her now?"

"Because, now she poses a threat to our lifestyle."

"How so?"

"She is not like us. When the time comes to fight, what will she do? And she will want to leave, she will want more answers."

"We can lie, make up some story... eventually she will give up on leaving."

"She won't give up, angel. She will find out what we are and why we are here, and when she does, she will become our enemy."

"If she becomes a problem, we will kill her, but right now she is not a problem." I stare him down, making it clear that I will not budge.

August sighs again and turns his back to me. He walks to the window and looks out over the expanse of trees. "You are one of a kind angel," says August.

I walk up behind him and wrap my arms around his waist, resting my cheek against his back.

"It's not that I'm *totally* against killing her, it's just that I think she could be useful."

"Oh?"

I can feel him shiver at my touch – he is just as easy to manipulate as any other man, it seems.

"She doesn't belong here, so why is she here? There is a reason, and we need to keep her alive until we find out."

He doesn't speak for several minutes while I hold on to him. Finally, I release him and he turns to face me.

"OK, we keep her alive for now." He smiles

a wicked smile and leans into me.

I think at first he is going to kiss me, but instead, he bends down to my cheek and nibbles me softly with his teeth. The sensation give me shivers, along with a pinch of fear. It is a reminder that this man is not simply human; he is a dangerous predator that I will never be safe with.

"What happened to you? Why did you leave?" I ask touching his ripped shirt.

"I needed to think things over," he says blankly.

Something in his expression lets me know that pushing him is a bad idea. It feels like he is simply humoring me.

I do not argue when he orders me to go to sleep that night. Throughout the night I wake to see him alternating between watching me and going to check on Hayley. He does not trust that she will stay, or that she will not kill us in our sleep.

Before the sun rises above the trees, I wake to see August lying beside me, watching me in the dim light. I am beginning to doubt that he even sleeps at all.

"Good morning."

"Good morning, angel." He stretches his hand out and touches my cheek.

"You can call me Lilith you know."

"No," he says seriously, and then moves on. "We need to discuss what we are going to tell your friend."

"We tell her that this place is isolated, and that there is no chance anyone will come for us. We tell her that we are prepared to stay here forever, and she should do the same. We tell her there is no way out."

"OK, then." August sits up. He is already dressed in his slacks and white button up, belt, shoes, and tie all in place.

"I'm going to go down and give her the news, you are welcome to come along, of course," says August in a businesslike tone.

"Oh yes, I would enjoy that so much, thank you, sir," I mock him, getting up and pulling my sweater over my t-shirt.

He grins and begins his descent. I finish dressing, and grab a couple of apples from the fruit basket before heading down myself.

I am halfway down the path when I hear a

scream so loud that it travels down my spine and gives me a sick feeling in my stomach.

I run as fast as I can down the path until I come to the canopy where I see August holding Hayley in his arms on the ground. She is bleeding from her wrist badly. Blood is flowing between August's fingers as he tries to put pressure on the wound.

"I'm sorry Lily, I just can't do this," Hayley sobs.

"Rip off some of that bedding," August orders me, and I do so without hesitation.

As I hand him the shredded cotton, a sick idea comes into my mind. *Had August talked her into this?* He did want her dead after all. *But why wouldn't he just kill her himself?*

"Here, stay with her, keep pressure on the wound," says August as he bolts off into the trees.

"Where are you going!?" I yell after him, but he does not reply.

Hayley has her eyes closed, she appears to be unconscious. I hold fast to the blood-soaked fabric, and suddenly the feeling comes back.

My emotions start to slip away, I am

empty, and peaceful, and I don't care for Hayley, I don't even care for myself. It is the most wonderful feeling, or lack thereof. Though I could simply let go of her wrist, for some reason I hold on tighter. There is no reason to keep her alive, but my instincts prevent me from letting go.

All of a sudden, I feel a sharp pain in my back and I turn to see a long dart sticking out of my sweater. Before I can reach for it the world has started to fade. I try desperately to hold onto Hayley's wrist, but weakness spreads through my body, too strong to fight.

I collapse on the ground, and before my eyes close I see a group of people in black tactical gear storming the clearing with their guns held high.

FIVE

"Wake up angel, it's go time!" The voice seems familiar, but everything is so foggy I can't see. It is loud, and every sound echoes inside my head.

"Wakey, wakey!" Finally, my brain connects the voice to my memories, it is August and he is shaking my arm.

I try to open my eyes further, but my eyelids feel like cement blocks. Suddenly, I am lifted into the air, floating, or flying, without any effort on my part. In my dreamy state I wonder if I really am an angel. A loud bang pushes my eyelids up and then I see fire, I can feel the warmth of it on my skin. I glance around and recognize the building is a hospital, tables have been turned over and bodies lie dead on the ground. It looks like a scene of war, I can find nobody alive within my view point.

"Where are we?" I ask, my voice cracking.

"We are about to be free," says August, carrying me toward the end of the hall.

The smoke makes me cough, and I wonder if August had set the fire himself. I can feel August limping as he carries me – he has been injured, though I can see little of him in the dim light.

It appears that the electricity in the building is out, and the only light source comes from the scattered fires that we pass in the hallway.

Finally, we burst through the doors at the end of the hall, and sunlight hits us. The rays are so powerful that even with my eyes closed, my head pounds in response. I can feel that August is running now. I open my eyes again when I feel shade on my face. There are trees above me, I see August focused straight ahead, his face bloody, and his breathing hard.

"Can you walk?" He asks, slowing.

"I think so," I reply, trying to move my legs. He puts me on the ground and steadies me with his hands.

My legs feel shaky, but they hold up nonetheless. I take in August's appearance; he is wearing only his underwear, and his entire body is streaked with blood and dirt. His thigh has a small wound where blood trickles slowly down to his knee.

I myself am wearing only a hospital gown. I feel dizzy and weak from the drugs they had no doubt been using to keep me sedated. I have so many questions that I want to ask, but I know there is no time.

"Let's go," August says, leading me by the hand through the trees.

I have no idea where we are in relation to the zoo, or how we will find our way out of the trees, but August pushes through the foliage as though he knows exactly were to go.

I expect to hear sirens, or the sound of someone chasing us, but I hear nothing, apart from August's heavy breathing, and our combined footsteps on the crunchy leaves.

The cold air makes my skin tingle and my body shiver. I am beginning to feel thankful for my ignorance, and for the haste we make through the forest. It gives me no time to be afraid, or to question what has happened.

After several minutes of silent walking, we stop at the edge of a creek. August is breathing harder than ever, leaning against a tree for support.

"Are you OK?" I ask.

"Cheeky as ever."

"Did you do all of that on your own?"

He laughs and looks at me. "Are you surprised?"

"I can't say that I am."

"All that matters is that we are alive, and we can continue to do what we were born to do."

"If we live long enough to get out of here and find supplies."

"I know where we are, don't worry. I've done my research."

"Why is a hospital out here?" I ask.

"It's not a public hospital. It's used as part of the zoo. Not nearly as big as you think, it was easy enough to clear out."

"What about Hayley?"

"She's one of them," says August.

"What do you mean?! Why would they put one of their own in there?"

"How should I know?"

"Well you seem to know everything else," I say, staring at him in shock.

"We don't have time to discuss everything now. Help me get across that creek so we can find somewhere safe before night."

Thankfully, the creek is a shallow one, with many rocks for us to cross on. August is running out of energy, his wound putting tremendous strain on his body. I can see him grimace with each step.

Once across the creek, he leans on me as we walk uphill through the forest, putting more distance between us and the hospital.

"I'm certain they will send men after us when they find out what I did to the hospital," August says as we walk. "So it's essential that we keep moving."

A cool breeze hits us when we crest the hill. I had hoped that the vantage point would offer us a better view, or some clue as to where we are. But the trees are thick, and I can see nothing beyond a few feet in front of us.

"Don't worry, angel," August says noticing my tense muscles.

"What if we can't get you to the hospital on time?" I say as the weight of our situation comes down on me.

"Does this mean you care for me, angel?"

"I just can't let you die after all you have done to keep me alive," I say truthfully.

He does not speak after that for a long time. I am worried beyond anything I have ever felt, and it is all for this creature that I fear.

I know that the reason I care for him is not some romantic fate, but the fact that he understands who I am more than anyone else can. August knows what I am, and accepts it without question because for him my devilish need to kill is familiar and comfortable.

Just as the sun is setting, and my worry increases tenfold, the sound of cars humming in the distance makes my knees weak.

"We are nearly there," says August.

The hope of finding civilization gives me a whole new burst of energy. Suddenly, the trees clear, and there it is; a long stretch of highway that goes on in a straight line, left and right until I can no longer see it. Tall pines line the sides of the road, giving it a deserted feel. Wind brushes against us, much colder now as the sun bows down behind the horizon.

"Now what do we do?" I ask.

"We wait for someone to pick us up," August replies.

And that is exactly what we do – me in my hospital gown, and August in his gray, Calvin Klein underwear. It all seems so funny, the sheer weirdness of the situation makes me laugh out loud.

"What is it angel?" August asks.

"Look at us!?"

He looks down and smiles. "Well, we will have no trouble getting the attention of passersby."

The two of us laugh until we see headlights crest the hill. August limps into the middle of the road, and at first I am afraid that the car will hit him, but the screeching breaks halt the vehicle a few feet away from him. *We are safe at last.*

Six

I wake up in a hospital bed and take note of my surroundings, quickly devising a plan of escape. My hands are bound – no surprises there. The room is a passionless off-white color, and there is a sense of deja vu surrounding this place.

I strain against the leather straps that hold my wrists and ankles to no avail. I look for items in the room – anything possibly useful. A plastic cup, a bed pan, a gown hanging from the door by a wire hanger, a box of tissues.

I lay my head against the pillow and breath in, then out. My muscles are sore, I try to think of the last moments before I passed out.

Blood, there was a lot of that. I had not planned on the girl doing my job for me. It had worked nonetheless, her family stepped in to save her. It was the last straw, they would not leave her to die in the zoo, no matter how screwed up the family may be.

I think back to the moment by the fire. That was when I realized killing the angel would not be enough, it would never be enough.

That kiss had revealed to me something extraordinary. *I am being played by a woman for the first time in my life.* I ponder this while I listen for footsteps from the hallway outside my room. It is dead silent. Perhaps the Beringer's are deciding what to do with me.

The big question is, of course, will I rescue the angel from the zoo? Or will I leave her to fend for herself. There is no doubt in my mind that this plan will work, and I will succeed in my escape. *I will kill Royal O'Conner.*

But as for her, I want to see her live. I want to see her punished for tricking me into a state of unexplored emotional territory.

However, leaving her to the punishing hands of the Beringer family could mean I miss out on the action. I thrash against the restraints again, harder this time. *How foolish of them to use leather.*

I struggle until I feel my skin tear, the pain inspiring me to complete my mission. The leather gives slightly, and suddenly my hand is free. Blood pours onto the white bed sheets. Quickly, I use my bloodied hand to undo the remaining cuffs.

Once freed, I move quickly to snatch the gown from the door, taking only the wire hanger. I untie it and straighten it out, this is my only weapon. Pressing my ear to the door, I listen hard – I will not move from this spot until I hear something.

And to my displeasure, I hear the cough of a man right outside. They have placed at least one guard here, maybe two if they know me at all.

The window is barred, the door is my only

way out, and it is surely locked. I consider trying the doorknob, but that would reveal my position. All of a sudden, I hear footsteps and I cannot believe my luck. I duck into the corner and wait. First there is a shadow at the bottom of the door, and some chatter between unknown people. Next, the door clicks and a woman steps in.

In an instant, I have the wire around her neck, turning her toward the door I use her as a human shield. The guard behind her is frozen with his hand on his gun belt.

"Put it down," I order.

The guard complies removing his gun. Without warning he raises it and fires, the excruciating pain in my leg is evidence that he is a terrible shot. I do not know if he hit the nurse, I throw her toward him with all my strength.

The woman screams, and the guard fires at me again, missing. The bullet punctures the wall behind me. I spin around and kick the gun out of the man's hands – it flies across the room, sliding into the opposite corner.

He swings at me, his face shocked. I dodge

his fist with ease and provide an answering attack that lands hard on his jaw. He takes one, two, then three steps backwards and falls to the ground, unconscious.

Meanwhile, the woman is crawling across the floor to the gun in the corner, but I stop her well before she reaches it. I grab her by the hair and pull her to the bed, where I strap her down with the same leather straps I had been bound with. My blood is still fresh there, soaking the bedding.

I take the gun and without hesitation I eliminate three other people who had heard the gunfire and hid in the hallway. As I pass the rooms, I look for my angel, but it is not until the last door that I see her. She is unconscious, likely sedated. Just as I enter her room I hear people in the hall, so I slip behind the door without making a sound.

"August Eaton, please step out with your hands up," a male voice demands.

"Cooperate and you can still come out of this alive," another voice chimes in.

I dart across the hall to the opposite room. I would not have my angel die so easily in the crossfire.

"Move in," I hear one of the guards say and I prepare for the worst.

I hide behind the only solid piece of furniture in the room, a large industrial sink. Just then, the room is filled with flames. I cover my face with my already wounded hand, the sink shielding me from the worst of it.

When the flames die down I lean around the corner and fire a few shots, pulling back before the return fire can hit me.

Someone moans, and I hear the sound of a body hitting the floor. Through the bullet-storm I notice that the fire does not return. *Could that really have been a flame thrower*? I repeat my assault again, but this time I don't know if I hit anyone.

Then the room begins to fill with smoke, and I realize they are gassing me out. I take one last breath and think about my next move. My eyes fill with tears as the smoke engulfs me.

I make my move, running out from behind the sink, I look through the fog, firing my last three shots. I drop two more men, and then to my delight, my suspicions are answered.

A flamethrower sits on the ground near the body of the first man I had taken down. I slide across the floor to it. Another man emerges and begins to raise his gun, but I am faster. The man falls dead. Slowly, and with some effort, I rise up holding the flame thrower. Examining my leg, I notice it is only scratched, the bullet had not hit me straight on.

Out in the hall I begin to burn the bodies of the fallen men. I can feel my sanity slipping away. A phenomenal feeling of unhinged anger fills my body, and I am no longer in control. I do not destroy because of vengeance, or even passion – I destroy because it makes me *feel*.

-PART FIVE-
DOWNFALL

ONE

August quickly concocted a story for us once we made it to the hospital. We had been mugged, all our things stolen, and August had been stabbed in the scuffle. As for our clothing, August somehow convinced the staff that it was not suspicious, though how, I have no idea.

After a few phone calls, August secured us both clothing, cash, and passports. When his leg had been patched up, we were in a taxi, and on our own.

"Where are we going?" I ask once we are safely inside the cab.

He pauses looking at the cab driver. "Sir, do you have a pen and paper?"

With the skill only a cab driver can have, the man steers the car with his knee while leaning over to dig through the glove compartment. He returns moments later with a pen and notepad. August takes them and scribbles quickly on the pad, handing it over for me to read.

We are going to my beach home. We'll be safe there for a while.

I lean my head against his shoulder and watch the trees fly by the window. It feels so bizarre to simply leave the zoo and be able to take a taxi without being arrested. Somehow I feel like more of a criminal now than I had before.

Several minutes pass in the quiet back seat of the cab before August orders the driver to pull over. We step out into the warm sun and the cool breeze of autumn. August pays the driver, and then the two of us head down the cobble sidewalk, hand-in-hand.

I am free, but somehow I feel trapped. August had kept me safe inside the zoo. He had decided for some reason not to kill me, and I am thankful for it. But now that we are free of the enclosure, I feel trapped with him.

I am certain that if I suggest we part ways, he will become upset. I remember when I first arrived in the zoo, the way he had seemed so unhinged, and so unpredictable. There is no doubt in my mind that if I push him far enough, he will return to that state, and it will mean the end of my life.

We walk through a quaint little town of an unknown name. As we crest the hill in the center of town, the ocean comes into view – stunning and vast as ever, it is an overwhelmingly beautiful sight to see.

"Just this way," says August, leading me on.

"This is a lovely place," I say, squeezing his hand. I know exactly what to do to make him comfortable.

"I grew up here," He says.

Around the corner and into a

neighborhood we walk. The houses are not over-sized, but comfortably designed between *medium* and *too large to be cozy.*

The third house from the end of the street is our destination, a gray brick two story home with a garage and a neatly kept yard. He pulls the key from above the door and unlocks it. Stepping inside, I find that it is spotless, not a speck of dust anywhere.

"Wow, how do you keep it clean?" I ask, staring at the vaulted ceiling in the entryway.

"I hire people." He laughs, closing the door behind us and locking it.

A chill goes up my spine as I hear the lock click into place.

"How many houses do you own?" I ask.

"Um, four," says August, flipping on the lights as we walk through the house.

The kitchen is extraordinary, open and modern. It is exactly the kind of place I envisioned someone like August having. I long to see what his primary house looks, like if something like this is his *vacation* home.

I peep out of the glass doors and see an impressive swimming pool, it too appears perfectly maintained, with a hot tub and a waterfall.

"This will have to do until we can get out of the country. I have a house in London."

"London!?" I say, surprised. "Is it really necessary to leave the country?"

"Absolutely necessary," he says looking at me seriously. "We need to put as much distance between the Beringer family and the two of us as we can."

"But they have no proof of anything! They can't put us in jail."

"That is true, but they could come after us, try to put the zoo back together again."

I can't think up a way to talk him into staying, but I am *not* going to England with him.

"When do we leave?" I ask, trying to sound eager.

"As soon as I tie up a few loose ends."

"What loose ends?" I ask. He seems irritated by my questions.

"You are relentless." He touches my cheek.

"I'm sorry," I say smiling.

"There is a man in the city that I need to

take care of."

"You mean *kill,* right?"

"Yes, *kill.*"

"What did he do?" I ask casually.

"He put me in the zoo," says August.

"I thought you liked the zoo," I chuckle.

"I don't like that he knows about who I am. It's not safe to let him live."

He turns his back to me, and walks to the kitchen. My heart leaps; perhaps this will be my chance to get away.

If he would just leave me, and go take care of his *unfinished business,* I could leave and he would never find me. Though I feel excited at the prospect of escaping, something in the pit of my stomach feels sickened by the idea. August has done nothing wrong to me, in fact, he is the only true friend I have.

However, I am aware that someone like me can never keep a friend and hope to stay alive, or stay out of prison long enough to enjoy my life. I have an important decision to make, and it is not going to be easy.

Part of me thinks that maybe if I stay with August, he will protect me, we can protect each other and the two of us could make a life together somewhere far away. Deep down, I know how foolish this dream is.

Two

I lie on top of the fluffy down comforter in Augusts beach house. The moonlight is shining through the open window, casting shapes on the ceiling. I listen to August's breath, he is fast asleep on the other side of the bed – one hand trailing behind him, settling on my arm. Even as he sleeps I feel him watching.

I am in a constant state of restlessness, because I know time is running out for me. I have to find a way out of this man's grasp for good, and I have to do it quickly before he realizes my true feelings.

The fact, is I do not love August Eaton, and I will not pretend to be anything more than a very strange acquaintance. His fingers move over my arm in his sleep and my heart stutters. Angry, I get up and go to the bathroom, where I let my hands sit under the hot water until it hurts.

"*I. Do. Not. Feel. Emotion,*" I whisper to myself in the mirror. My mahogany hair is flowing down across my face, making me look gaunt.

A memory from my childhood comes back and I cringe away from it. I had not thought about that day in years. I try hard to repress it, but the image of my sisters tiny coffin floods my brain.

I pull at my hair the way I used to, the pain distracting me from the memory – my heart steadies. I turn it off and move back to the bedroom. *I cannot go back to bed,* I think looking at August's muscular back. He looks so powerful, even while sleeping.

I think about walking out the door, but fear keeps me. He grunts in his sleep, and his arm twitches as though responding to my thoughts. I worry that the only way I am getting out of here is *dead.*

I form a plan as I watch the sun rise through the sliding-glass doors. August had mentioned unfinished business with a stranger, something that kept him from leaving the country immediately. This means that August has a serious enemy, one that needs him out of the way just as much as I do.

If I can find this enemy before August, and get him on my side, I have a chance of escaping unharmed, and for good. It will not be easy. August is a careful, and intelligent man. He will not let information go haphazardly, even to me. But he trusts me, at least a little, and I can use that trust to gain an advantage.

"So who is he?" I ask, leaning against the bar while August prepares breakfast.

He does not respond, poking a fork at the bacon sizzling in the pan. He is shirtless, and I worry he'll burn himself. I ignore my own stupidity.

"It's fine if you don't want to tell me, I just thought it would be easier if I'm going to help."

"His name is Royal O'Conner," he spits at me, frustrated. *Maybe this will be easier than I thought.*

"Are you mad at me?" I say, changing the subject. I make a mental note – *Royal O'Conner.*

"Of course not, angel," says August smiling wide, and I believe him. It is incredible how believable he is. Whether telling the truth or not, I always *want* to believe him.

"So what can I do to help?"

"Firstly, we have to make absolutely certain that he is still living in the same house. Then, we get his schedule, and we take him when nobody is looking." August removes a strip of bacon from the grease, laying it on the pristine white plate.

"Does he have a family?" I ask.

"No family," says August, smiling.

The conversation pauses while he starts work on the eggs. I watch him cook and think of a plan.

"Maybe I could do some research on him, find out where he's living now," I suggest.

"If you want," he says, flipping an egg. "Thank you for being my partner in this."

His eyes are convincing, but his expression falters for a moment, but it is almost instantly restored. I think I see something fake, but it feels like my mind playing tricks.

"I wouldn't want to be anywhere else," I say smiling, trying to believe my own words.

THREE

Pressing enter on the keypad of the prepaid cellphone, I count the rings until he answers.

One.

Two.

Three.

"Are you alone?"

"Yes, but only for a few minutes."

"You have to find a way to get him out of the house."

"And how will I do that?"

"Tell him you have an informant, one that

will only talk in person. Say that he wants to meet you somewhere. Make it up, but make it convincing. August is not stupid, if he starts suspecting you, we're done."

"OK, I'll do what I can. Wait for my text." The call ends with a beep.

August is sleeping in the next room, but I am wide awake. I am always awake these days, so this behavior is not at all suspicious. I keep the calls short, I speak quietly from across the house in the entryway by the front door. *August is oblivious.*

The prepaid phone is one that August bought for me, so we can keep in touch if we get separated while carrying out our plan to murder Royal. He doesn't know that I am using the phone to plan against him – a*nd what a plan it is.*

When I first spoke with Royal O'Conner, he was not as surprised as I thought he would be – finding out that August is still alive, and now a free man. When August and myself had made our escape, someone had contacted Royal, and in turn he had fled for his own safety. I am only able to talk to him over the phone, and getting his number was no easy task.

The disposable phone has been useful during my stay at the beach home. Nearly as soon as August had given it to me, I called my parents to let them know I was safe. To my surprise, they were hardly worried. I expected tears of relief, but found them cheery and happy to hear from me.

"That note was a little rude," my mother had said when I called.

"Note?"

"The one you left telling us that you were going on vacation with your friends. I would have thought you would tell us in person, maybe even ask permission..."

The Beringer family had covered all the bases, though I wonder what my parents would have done if I had never come home from that vacation...

August emerges from the bedroom just as the sun is rising. He is fully dressed and ready for the day. Even though most days we spend indoors, pouring over information provided by August's contacts, he always dresses well. Tie, shirt, pants, belt, jacket, right down to the polished shoes. Sometimes he takes the jacket off and lays it across the back of the chair. *His casual look.*

"I want to go home and get some of my things," I say in my most demanding tone.

"What things?" He replies, raising an eyebrow.

"I need a certain item, if we are going to be killing anyone." I turn around in the fluffy white arm chair to get a better look at him.

"Is this part of your ritual?"

"Yes," I say, and he seems to understand.

"What about your family? I'm assuming you lived with them before you disappeared."

"They are not worried about me. You can come too, pretend to be my rich boyfriend." I wink at him playfully.

"I can't see a reason not to go" says August, shrugging. "Why not go now?"

"Now?"

He grins. "Yes. Get ready."

I hurry to the bedroom and take out one of the dresses August had bought me. Suddenly, I feel excited to show off my handsome, wealthy boyfriend. I wonder if my family will disapprove – he *does* look much older than me. And then I realize I don't know how old he is at all.

"How old are you?" I say at the entrance to the kitchen as I pull on my shoes.

"Thirty-four," he says curiously. "Why?"

I grimace, and then recover. "Can we say you are twenty-four?"

"You think I can pass for twenty-four?" He snickers.

I look him over – he does not look thirty-four, but he does not look twenty-four either.

"Twenty-eight, then," I say with a simper.

"OK." He approaches me. "My name is August Eaton, I am twenty-eight years old. Nice to meet you, Mr. and Mrs. Kane." He extends his hand and shakes mine. I marvel at his convincing face.

"Wait, how do you know my name?"

"I've known your name since before you arrived at the zoo, *Lilith.*" He smiles, and there is a hint of danger as he says my name. Goosebumps raise on my arms.

"Did they tell you? The Beringer's?"

"Yes." He touches my cheek with his thumb. "I expect you won't mention our business to your parents."

"Of course not," I say, severely.

"Good," says August, moving in to nibble my cheek with his teeth. I shiver again.

It takes us two hours from the beach house to get to my parents sleepy neighborhood. When we arrive, my parents cars are both in the driveway. August pulls his white BMW in front of the house, and we wait for a moment before getting out. August is following my lead, allowing me to take my time.

"Lilith!" My mother shrieks when she opens the door. "Carl! Lilith is home!" She shouts over her shoulder, dragging me into a hug.

When she pulls away, my mother is staring at August with wide eyes. I can see her looking around him at the car we had arrived in.

"Mom, this is my boyfriend, August," I say getting nervous. It feels dumb calling him my boyfriend, when p*artner in crime* seems more fitting.

"August Eaton, pleasure to meet you Mrs.

Kane." August presents an award-winning smile that is impossible to ignore. Charm oozes from him effortlessly. My mother's body language changes, she is taken in by him instantly, smiling and blushing.

"Nice to meet you too, August."

"Hey there!" My dad booms as he joins us in the entryway.

He looks at August with incredulous eyes. "And who is this?" He says, reaching out his hand.

"August Eaton." August flashes another smile – it doesn't seem to be as potent with my father.

"This is my boyfriend, daddy," I say in a sweet voice.

"Oh, nice to meet you."

"Nice to meet you too sir."

"How about we all go into the kitchen?" My mother says, taking my father by the hand.

"I just need to use the bathroom," I say.

"Of course," says August, following my parents to the kitchen.

As soon as the bathroom door is shut, I

take out my phone and text Royal.

The house is empty. You have two hours. Good luck.

I return a few minutes later and take the seat beside August at our family table. He looks so strange sitting in our relaxed country-style kitchen, his fingers interlaced on top of a duck-printed place mat.

"So, did you two meet on vacation?" My mother gushes, looking at August.

"We had met previously, through a mutual friend. But we met again on vacation, yes."

"How nice. And what do you do for a living?" My mother asks.

"I'm a screenwriter."

"Oh, wow! For movies?"

"Yes, mostly."

"That is exciting! Carl, he writes movies!" She bumps my father with her elbow, and he shoots her a dirty look.

"That's impressive," he says staring at August. "Listen, I need to cut to the chase here." My father leans forward, elbows on the table.

"Now, Carl..."

"Shh, Nancy, please." He puts a hand on her arm. "I can tell from your body language that you are not leaving here without my daughter. This is just a visit, I know she isn't staying. But how am I supposed to feel about that when I know nothing about you?"

August smiles a warm, friendly smile. "Mr. Kane, I have taken very good care of your daughter during our time together, and I will continue to do so. If she wants to stay with me then I will not argue, you will simply have to take it up with her."

I get a lump in my throat, this is where I'm supposed to respond, but all I can do is stare at August.

"Well, kiddo? What's the plan?" My parents are watching me, and so is August.

"I uh... I am going to be staying with August. It's closer to the beach, and I'd like to be there when classes start," I say with a shaky voice.

"So you are leaving us..." my mother says, disappointed.

"I will make her visit every week." August touches my mother's hand, and she adjusts in her seat. My dad looks leery.

"There are a few things I need to get from my room while I'm here," I add. My phone beeps, and August looks at me. "Probably a wrong number," I say.

Four

The car ride home is mostly quiet. The black trash bag full of my stuff is perched on the back seat, sliding back and forth on the leather as we turn corners. I reach behind and fumbled with the bag until I find my white rabbit mask. Holding it, I examine the chipped paint on the pink eyes.

"That is your ritual?" August asks.

"Yes, I wore this the first time I killed, and I've worn it every time since."

"How many times?"

"Twelve, counting the one in the zoo," I say. August smiles.

"Who was your first?"

"My sister." I try to seem calm, but my insides are churning. August does not respond.

When we arrive at the beach house, I haul my stuff inside and begin putting everything away. I want to look around to see if Royal moved anything. I need to make sure it looks like it did when we left, but August is watching me, he is *always* watching me. The only freedom I get comes with those few hours in the night, when August sleeps and I watch the moon.

"Why don't we go out for dinner," August says, pushing away from the table where he is writing an email.

"That would be nice," I say, eagerly – this will give Royal another opportunity to set up the scene.

"Great. Seven o'clock?" He suggests, and I agree.

I go into the bathroom to get ready, expecting August to follow me as he usually does, but this time he keeps his seat at the table. He doesn't even look at me when I pass. *Strange.*

"I'm going to get ready," I say, perplexed.

"OK," he says, going back to his email. I take this rare alone time to text Royal.

Going out for dinner tonight.
Be here at 7:30.
Take no longer than an hour.

I send the message, and then delete it. I shower and get dressed after that, feeling anxious about the plan. August is being more lenient than normal, and this makes me worry. His behavior could mean he is trusting me more, or it could mean something bad.

"You look great," says August, looking at my simple white dress. I've tied my hair up in a tight bun – elegant and clean, just as he likes.

"Thank you," I say. I know exactly how good I look, and I am hoping that it distracts him from my solicitous mood.

"Ready?" He says, standing.

I nod and follow him out the door. He

turns out the lights as he goes and locks the door behind him.

August opens the door for me and I take my seat in the passenger side of his beautiful white BMW; it still smells new. He backs out of the driveway, and keeps backing out. We go speeding down the street backwards, my heart flying. He screeches to a halt on the curb, parked so that we can see only the driveway of his house.

"What's going on!?" I say, alarmed.

"Give me your phone," he says, calmly.

"Why?" I say, reaching for the car door.

He grabs my arm and I know I cannot escape. We look at each other for a moment – he is daring me to make a move.

I calmly reach into my caramel-colored clutch, and hand him the phone. There is nothing on the phone, all calls and messages have been deleted. I relax a little at the thought.

He turns it on and begins typing quickly, then he throws the phone onto my lap, staring forward. I glance at the screen and see a text message to Royal. It simply says:

Move now. All clear.

I swallow hard. He is going to kill Royal, and it is all my fault. *I. Do. Not. Feel. Emotion.* I chant in my mind, my hands shaking against my knees. August is still holding onto my arm, his fingers like a vice, turning the skin beneath them white.

"I don't know what's happening," I say.

"Don't pretend with me, angel."

"I'm just scared, please don't do this."

"This has nothing to do with you. If you had just stayed out of it..." His fingers tighten on my arm. "Ticktock, *tick...*"

The wildness in his eyes comes back, the same madness I saw the first day we met. He takes my hand and nibbles the tip of each finger. I closed my eyes, fear digging down into my stomach.

"I should have set you free," says August, dropping my hand and giving me one cold look before turning away.

A few minutes later, I see a rusty old car pull into August's driveway. I can feel my heart pounding in my ears. August puts the car in drive and we move slowly back to the beach house.

By the time we get there, the car is empty, and the front door is slightly ajar. I grab the phone in my lap and cling to it. If there is a moment where August is distracted I can call the police.

"Get out," August orders, and I surrender.

He grabs my arm again and marches me to the front door. To my surprise, he removes a gun from his pocket, a compact semi-automatic.

I can feel a bead of sweat running down the side of my face. He cracks open the door and the two of us barge in, my heels making a loud clacking noise on the tile floor. I hear scuffling as the intruder attempts to hide.

"I have a gun, and I have surveillance cameras. Come out now, and I *might* not call the police." There is a moment of silence, and then a loud bang. The gunshot takes a chunk out of the wooden door frame, and sends both of us to the ground. I catch sight of a man hidden behind the bar – a dark shape in the shadows. August turns the corner and fires his gun into the dark house. I can hear the man wailing – August has hit his mark.

"Come on," August says, picking me up by the elbow.

He flicks on the lights, and there in a pool of blood on the floor, is a man I've never seen, though I know he must be Royal O'Conner.

"Tell me exactly why you are here," August says, pointing the gun at the man's face.

He coughs and blood trails from his mouth, dripping down onto his Hawaiian shirt.

"Tell me, or I kill you."

There is a moment of silence. The two men stare each other down.

"I'm here... *to kill you*," the man says through labored breathing.

"Who sent you?"

"Royal... O'Conner... and... her," he gasps again, pointing at me.

"Wha-what?!" I stumble over my words.

"Take the phone out, and call him," August commands. My hands shake as I dial the number. August rips the phone out of my hand before I can put it to my ear.

"Call this even, and be grateful I'm not killing you, or the girl," August speaks softly, and then hangs up.

I see the numbers *911* appear on the phone, and my heart does a back flip. My mind is on a roller coaster ride. August is framing me for attempted murder, and there is nothing I can do about it.

-PART SIX-
THE LAST

ONE

I take the pocket watch out and stare at it. The time matches the digital time on my phone perfectly. I let the satisfaction settle in – *at least something is going right in my life.*

I look out the window at the tarmac below – a man directing planes shuffles by looking bored. I curl my fingers around the cup of coffee. I opted for a mocha today in the place of my usual skinny latte. Sometimes life surprises me, and when it does, I need a little something special. It was so easy to predict her motives. She was beautiful, yes, she was perfection, but she was also my weakness. I had allowed her to live long passed what I should have, and even now, she lives on out of my hands. I see words forming beneath the foam in my mocha.

You failed.

I swallow a lump in my throat, *the words are true*. My destiny is to free angels like Lilith Kane, and I couldn't do it for my own selfish reasons. I want to see her suffer in prison right along with Royal O'Conner for even entertaining the idea of manipulating me.

From the start I knew about her plan – as if I wouldn't catch those late night texts, or phone calls. It is simple to trace someone's activity if you have the power, and I certainly do. I barely even needed the help of my lawyer to frame them both for attempted murder. The video evidence, the text messages, the drugs in her parents house, and in her car.

At first, I was devastated, betrayed by my own property, but I got over it. I learned that vengeance is almost as much fun as killing. I have to admit, the entire experience has been great for my confidence. I've learned to overcome what cannot be controlled, and take the higher road – *be the better man.*

The evidence I had stacked against them held up even better than I thought in court, which was a nice surprise. My lawyer was pleased with the success of our case.

We played Lilith off as a cheating girlfriend who was playing me for the money, and then using that money for drugs, all the while having a relationship with my business acquaintance, *Royal O'Conner.*

The two of them planned to have me killed, they even hired a hit man to come to my house. Luckily, I was armed and able to defend myself. The attempted murder charge, plus the drug possession, was enough to give them considerable sentences. I know one day they will get out of prison, and when they do, *I will kill them.*

The pocket watch ticks on in my hands. I like the feeling of its gears turning, it feels like a tiny heartbeat, keeping perfect time with my world. I have forty minutes until my plane boards. I look around the airport coffee shop, people are lined up to get their caffeine, others sit on laptops enjoying the free Wi-Fi.

A man sitting at the table opposite me gets up and walks away, only to have his chair filled by another man. A booming laugh erupts from my chest before I can stop it. People are staring, but I don't care. I lean forward clutching my ribs, laughter all but pushing me to the floor.

"Hello, August," Joe Beringer says coolly. "It is time to go home."

About The Author

BRITTNEY STEWART is the author of *The Last of the Dying*, a NaNoWriMo (see nanowrimo.org) 2009 winning novel. Brittney was born and raised in Oklahoma where she lives and writes today. Visit **www.brittneystewart.com**

UNUSUAL PUBLISHING

facebook.com/
brittneystewartbooks

@brittneybooks on twitter